# HER DIRTY ROCKERS

## A MEN AT WORK REVERSE HAREM NOVEL

### MIKA LANE

HEADLANDS PUBLISHING

# COPYRIGHT

# BE THE FIRST TO KNOW...

Want more heat, heart,
and bad boys who know what they're doing?
Join my list and I'll send the steam straight to your inbox,
starting with a deliciously naughty story:

SIGN UP TO MY MAILING LIST!
Or visit:
https://geni.us/free-book-signup

# CORAL

"You want me to do *what*?"

My boss Randall, in his unfortunately crooked toupee, leaned back in his desk chair, hands behind his head, smiling from ear to ear.

He was throwing me a bone. I should be grateful. Bones were good. *Most* bones, anyway.

I had no idea how I would tell him that this one was not.

"Coral, why aren't you excited about this new client? You should be jumping up and down and screaming, not to mention thanking me with a big, grateful hug."

I'd completely baffled him.

And he was right to be. I should have been on cloud nine, having been assigned the most high-profile client our public relations firm had ever landed. If I did a good job, this would catapult me into the company spotlight. The journalists I pitched stories to would actually take my calls. The firm would land more high-paying celebrity clients.

Which was the pinnacle of success for any Los Angeles-based PR firm. Big clients begat other big clients. The old snowball effect.

And I could see the dollar signs in Randall's eyes. Not that he didn't deserve all the success that came his way. The man had worked his fingers to the bone since starting the firm at his kitchen table, representing a little consortium of West Hollywood businesses. Word got around that he was good at what he did, and boom, his firm was born. Small and mighty, but absolutely respectable, he'd been toiling for ten years, waiting for that one client who'd hurl him into the top echelon of LA firms.

It looked like that time had come.

And he wanted me to handle the client. All by myself. Like a big girl.

I shook the doubts away.

It didn't work.

"Um, oh, Randall, I am totally grateful. You have no idea what this vote of confidence means to me. Seriously. It's an honor. You know I appreciate it."

Big lies, all of them.

I swallowed the bitterness rising in my throat. I needed water, now.

Clapping his hands together, he leaned forward on his desk. "Super. You'll meet with them tomorrow."

Something slammed against the recesses of my stomach, and if I hadn't been in front of my boss, I would have doubled over and groaned.

Oh god help me.

"Thank you, Randall," I said, forcing my voice to sound like something more than a thin squeak.

He furrowed his brow. He was no dummy.

"What's the hesitation, Coral? Anything I need to know? I chose you for this assignment because you're the best the firm has. You get results like no one else. This will be good for the firm. For us. For *you*."

I smiled and nodded, grappling for the enthusiasm he wanted to see.

I straightened up in my chair to show how serious I was. "I'm thrilled, Randall. Just nervous about doing such high-profile work," I lied again. "Everyone will be watching. But that's a good thing. We can handle this. *I* can handle this."

He beamed. "That's the Coral I know and love. You'll knock it out of the park, I know you will. And hey, I'm going to be right beside you all the way. We're partners in this."

"G... great. This is so great," I chirped.

Oh mother of god. I had no idea what I was going to do.

I needed time. Yes, I would buy time. Think carefully about what I would say.

He raised a finger. "Oh. Almost forgot the best part."

Oh, goody.

"If this goes well, I want you to become a partner in the firm."

What? Did he just say something about becoming a partner?

Holy shit.

"You're speechless, Coral. Never thought I'd see that." He laughed.

Neither did I.

*Me?* A *partner?* In the *firm?*

It was what I'd hoped for since the day I started. I'd worked my ass off because one, I loved the work, and two, because I knew that moving up the ladder would be rewarding on many levels, not least of which was financial. And after the way I'd grown up, with my parents just squeaking by, I was pretty motivated by the almighty dollar. I couldn't lie. I had regular nightmares about my staggering student loans.

But even more important, I'd be a *success*. A bona fide success at the level no one ever thought I'd be.

The doubters could suck it.

Wait till I told Nikki, my BFF. She was going to lose her shit. *She* was on my side. Had been for as long as we'd known each other.

Numb, I gave Randall one last smile and wandered back to my office to Google my new client, Dirty

Bandit. Not that I needed to Google the number one rock band in the world. Of course I knew who they were. Everyone did. The bad boys of rock. I'd kept an eye on their meteoric rise from garage band to stadium-filler.

This is what most everyone knew of them.

Enter *me*.

*I* knew these guys from before Dirty Bandit even existed.

Our association was not a happy one.

"Coral, one more thing," Randall said, sticking his head in my office. "Maybe you'll get some concert tickets out of this. Wouldn't that *rock?*"

Boss jokes. Almost as bad as dad jokes.

Anyway, like I would ever go to a Dirty Bandit concert. I hated rock 'n roll and I hated *their* music even more.

Randall shook his head at his pun, and turned to one of my coworkers in the hallway, where they began to discuss the shoe company we did PR for.

I needed to think, and fast. I had to concoct a reason why I couldn't possibly work with Dirty Bandit, the world's biggest rock band and the most prestigious client our firm had ever had.

'Course, I could always tell the truth.

No, scratch that.

Whatever I came up with, people would think I needed to have my head examined. But that was fine. I could weather that storm.

Working with Dirty Bandit, not so much.

Why couldn't *I* work on the shoe account, where all we did was make sure famous actresses wore our clients' shoes to award ceremonies and other events? So civilized. So easy. And all those free shoes.

It was amazing how, with just a few words, one could be transported from an imperfect but satisfying everyday existence to someplace so uncomfortable, it made your skin itch. I rubbed my forearms, but the creepy crawlies wouldn't go away.

My day had seriously gone to shit.

Was I overstating it?

Nope.

Before the end of the day, Randall would be getting a big, fat *no* from me.

One way or the other.

## CORAL

It was back in tenth grade when it started. I remember it like it was yesterday.

Why was it that the shitty stuff always stayed in the forefront of our minds, and the pleasant stuff slipped away, under-appreciated and easily forgotten?

Was it just me?

I'd been running down the hall, late for English because I'd taken too long to get cleaned up and dressed after gym class. I could have just stripped off my sweaty clothes next to my locker, showered, and gotten re-dressed like the other girls as soon as class had ended. But I never did that.

Instead, I procrastinated by hanging out in the gym

teacher's office, shooting the breeze with her about anything I could think of. I got a lump in my throat when I thought back to how kind she'd always been, so clearly aware of my awkwardness.

I wasn't about to change in front of my pretty, slim classmates, all gliding through adolescence with flat tummies, clear skin, and cool clothes from Forever 21.

While chatting up Mrs. Holloway about anything I could think of, I would watch, out of the corner of my eye, for when the first of the girls started to exit the locker room, fresh and clean, to head to their next classes. I'd say goodbye to my teacher and rush back to my locker to change lightning fast. This didn't leave but a couple of minutes to not only dress and put my towel in the laundry, but also scoot to my next class on the far side of the building.

Which meant I had to run.

But I'd been doing this since the beginning of the school year. I had my routine down pat.

Until the day one of the Populars decided to have some fun at my expense. The Populars, who were now the world-famous Dirty Bandit.

Yup, I'd grown up with those assholes.

As I was heading to Mrs. Siebert's English class, Stone, Ennis, and Hugh—now the band's front men— lounged along the school corridor with their other genetically and socially blessed friends. And just as I whipped around the corner with only seconds before the late bell rang, one of them extended his foot.

Right in my path.

My wipeout caused such a ruckus that Mrs. Siebert stuck her head into the hallway to see what was going on. As soon as she did, the snickering Populars slunk away to their classes, late as always, with not a care in the world.

After the initial pain in the knee I'd fallen on had migrated to my pride, I picked up my books and limped into class. Mrs. Siebert smiled at me kindly and had everyone open their textbooks while I got settled in, as if to give me a moment to compose myself.

I'd wanted to cry, of course. But I hadn't. Not then.

Why did I feel like crying now, ten years later?

What were the minuscule chances that after all these years I'd *see* these guys again, much less *work* with them—the nemeses of my high school years? In what freaking universe does a weird coincidence like that happen?

Apparently, mine.

Yes, I'd wanted success at the firm. Yes, I'd wanted to impress my boss with work on an important client.

But did I want to spend one second with three guys who had their heads so far up their asses they'd made me want to forget my teenage years like they were one long, bad dream?

They'd taken such pleasure in tripping me that day that they'd continued to subject me to their petty humiliations until we graduated.

So, my sweet revenge was to reinvent myself, become a success, and never set eyes on them again.

What was the likelihood that they'd make it in a town like Los Angeles, anyway, where every other kid has big plans for a rock star future?

Why'd *they* have to be the ones who rocketed to fame? Where was the fairness in that?

And where was the fairness in, years later, my having to take them on as a client?

I was, essentially, going to work for them.

The indignities I'd left behind?

*Hello! We're back!*

I'd started transforming myself the day after high school graduation as if there were no time to waste. I was heading to college and my old life was going to be pushed so far into the past, it would be like it had never happened. The summer between my senior year in high school and freshman year in college was going to be transformative. But not by accident. I knew there was work ahead.

I started riding my bike to the fast food restaurant where I was a cashier. No more hitching rides. I stopped eating burgers and fries, replacing them with salad. I ditched my glasses for contact lenses. I got highlights.

I bought some cool clothes at Forever 21 with my summer earnings.

I lost my virginity to the boy down the street who'd started showing an interest in me. It was not particularly memorable. Just something I wanted to get out of the way.

It had been a busy summer.

And so I embarked on a new, reinvigorated life, light years away from the jerks who'd looked down on me in high school.

Now they were back.

Did someone say life was fair?

Because it was not.

3

_______________


CORAL


"I was thinking, Randall..." I said, returning to his office and helping myself to a chair.

His walls were covered in photos of him meeting various celebrities. I knew they were chance meetings and that he didn't really know them. But I didn't let on. He deserved to have his fun.

He took a sip of his coffee. "Hey, Coral. You got some ideas for Dirty Bandit? You're meeting with them tomorrow. Aren't you excited?"

Good god. This wasn't going to be easy.

"Well, that's what I wanted to talk to you about."

He leaned forward on his desk, waiting for my pearls of wisdom.

Always a fan of *ripping off the bandage* when it came to bad news, I laid it on him with little hesitation. "Randall, I can't work on that account. I'm sorry. I really am."

Whew. I'd done it.

I sat back in my chair, waiting for him to fire me. Not that he was the firing type, but I'd never pushed him on anything like this before.

And I didn't want to be fired. But if that were the price to pay, so be it.

He studied me, clearly trying to figure out how to respond.

Would he cajole me, gently moving me toward the realization that yes, this was work I was longing to do?

Would he strong-arm me, threatening my future at the firm and rescinding his offer of potential partnership?

Or would he simply let me off the hook and assign Dirty Bandit to someone else in the office?

"Can you elaborate, Coral?" he asked patiently.

I took a deep breath. "Randall, I grew up with those guys. They aren't nice people."

His eyes widened. "No way. You already know them?" He grinned like he'd just won the lottery.

"Yeah, um, and in high school—"

He sprang to his feet and clapped his hands in glee. "Oh my god. It's meant to be," he cried.

This was not going how I'd planned.

"Randall, I'm not sure you heard me right—"

"This is incredible. Getting a high-profile client like this has been my dream for years. But your having a relationship with them? That's freaking perfect. I bet you broke all their hearts back then," he giggled. "They were probably all in love with you, huh?"

I think he had tears in his eyes.

I know I had tears in mine.

While Randall was imagining I'd been a high school heartbreaker, I was remembering the anxiety I'd suffered at the hands of those three Populars.

I'd lost then and it looked like I was about to lose again now.

I thought I'd left that shit behind. These days, I was smart. And sort of successful. And even a little pretty.

That awkward geek from Perry High School no longer existed.

So if she no longer existed, why did I feel like she was gaining ground on me, getting ready to spray-paint *loser* down the side of my freshly-washed Prius, just like there once had been down the front of my hall locker?

**4**

_______________

## STONE

The morning sun blinded the shit out of me as I emerged from the dingy, disgusting county jail. I pulled open the passenger door of Bryan's black Mercedes, closing it with that satisfying airlock thud that only cars of that caliber have.

"Dude, do you have any sunglasses I could borrow?" I asked, stuffing the personal items the jail had returned to me back into their usual pockets—phone, wallet, keys. I'd left my handful of coins in the bin they'd kept everything in. County could have it as a little token of my appreciation.

Bryan reached into his glove box as he navigated the car onto the busy LA freeway. "Here, take these.

They're scratched but they'll do. Where are your sunglasses?"

I shrugged. "One of the guards probably stole them. Wanted a little souvenir of Dirty Bandit. Those fuckers were all over me, wanting autographs and photos. I didn't get a wink of sleep."

But at least they'd given me my own jail cell.

For better or for worse, the guys at County knew me. And they'd never forget me, because after every 'visit,' I sent those bastards a case of whiskey.

Were they allowed to accept gifts like that? Hell no.

But the guards did whatever the fuck they wanted. Don't kid yourself. Those places were as lawless as the streets.

I looked out the car window and laughed. What a fucking contrast. From dirty cinder block walls, piss and blood-stained mattresses, and open-air shitters, to one of the most expensive Mercedes you could buy, flying down the road in quiet luxury, leaving slower cars in our dust.

It was like home after a shitty vacation. That was why I loved these cars, these pods of escapism. I had two of them myself.

I hadn't set out to get two cars. I had no interest in being one of those douchebags who owns cars just to own them. Most of the time I was transported around by a driver anyway.

But when my Benz was in the shop for a couple

days and I wanted to take a drive up the coast, I bought another one. Just like the first.

Different color, though.

That was about as douchebaggy as I got. Well, except for the fighting. I fought a lot. I didn't try to. It was like it sought me out. But being famous was not an invitation for every creep in town to touch me, talk to me, or photograph me.

And it didn't help that I had a big goddamn mouth.

I just wanted to be left alone. I had people coming at me all day, wanting something—a new and better song, a public appearance, an endorsement. Face time to make them feel important. But when the paparazzi stepped over the line, well, all bets were off. Unfortunately, my demands for privacy had bought me free overnights in jail twice this year.

Twice, so far.

Would there be more? Probably.

"I'm beginning to think you like jail food," Bryan said.

"Fuck off. You know I don't eat when I'm in County. Speaking of which, I'm starving. Will you swing by Nobu so I can get some sushi?"

Bryan steered the car toward the exit for West Hollywood. "All right. They're not open yet, though."

"Just go. They'll open."

We arrived to locked doors. As expected.

Yeah, no one served lunch at ten a.m. But I'd get in.

I always did.

Peering through the window into the dark restaurant, I knocked. There was movement in the kitchen, probably staff getting the place ready for the day. But as expected, no one came to the door. I knocked one more time, and when no one answered, I looked their number up on my phone.

"Nobu," an efficient voice said.

"Um, hey, this is Stone from Dirty Bandit. I'm out front. Can you let me in for a little lunch?"

The phone answerer hesitated. I knew she wanted to blow me off. They weren't ready for customers yet, and waiting on Bryan and me would throw off their morning prep.

If I'd heard it once, I'd heard it a hundred times.

But damn. I was really jonesing for Nobu. "Look, I'll pay twice the price. I'm just really craving Japanese. I had a rough night."

I checked my wallet, which was empty. It was always empty. That was what Bryan was for.

There was a sigh, and footsteps from inside grew nearer. Then the front door flew open. A small woman looked up and down the sidewalk and shooed us in before anyone else made the mistake of asking them to serve lunch two hours early. She was showing us to a table in a private-ish corner when the manager came flying out.

"Yo. Stone. Good to see you."

We did that guy half-shake, half-hug thing. He ignored Bryan.

People who worked for celebrities were used to being treated as if they were invisible. But if they were smart, they didn't let it bother them. They got paid a shit-ton of money to make up for the petty humiliation of living in somebody's shadow.

"Hey, thanks for letting us in. I just spent the night in County, and now I'm dying for something good to eat."

The manager smiled like he heard this story every day. "Dude. You want the usual?"

I nodded and gestured toward Bryan. "You know it. Bryan?"

"Same," he said, not looking up from his phone.

"Oh, and an Asahi Super Dry. Actually, two," I called after him.

Bryan rolled his eyes. "Really? Beer at ten a.m.?"

I started chowing on a bowl of edamame. "Whatever. Get a fucking Shirley Temple, if you prefer."

Bryan, bless his goddamn heart, had been with us since the beginning. And I mean the real beginning, back when we had to lug our own shit around and play in empty dive bars.

Thank god that period of our lives had been short-lived. It fucking sucked.

And now, truth be told, I couldn't imagine life without the man, as much as he was a major pain in my ass. But that's what we paid him for.

Like bailing me out of jail.

"So what happened?" he asked.

Here it comes.

"I don't know what you mean," I said, popping *uni* in my mouth. Fun fact. *Uni* were sea urchin testicles.

I didn't care. They were delicious.

He set his chopsticks down. "You know what I mean."

He was right. I did.

"To tell the truth, I don't really remember. I know there was a fight. It said so right on my release paperwork from County, and my hitting hand hurts like a bitch. Other than that, I'm not entirely sure."

"Fine," he said, narrowing his eyes. "Let me refresh your shitty memory. You started a bar brawl with someone who bumped into you when you were likely already three sheets to the wind. Problem is, that somebody works for your record label."

I waved my hand at the waiter, who was delivering more food. I was full. And I wanted to get the hell away from Bryan. I hated when he got on his bitch soapbox.

"You know what? People are goddamn crybabies. All of them."

I stood, signaling that lunch was over and that Bryan could pay.

Well, he wasn't *really* paying. He was using one of the band's credit cards.

Dude had just gotten a free lunch on me.

5

STONE

Don't you know, the second we walked out of Nobu, some punk paparazzi jumped in front of me and snapped a pic. I fucking hated that. But because I'd just gotten out of the slammer and Bryan was with me, I kept my mouth shut and my head down. I stuffed my hands in my pockets to control my swinging fists.

"Where to?" Bryan asked when we were back in the quiet calm of his car.

I looked out the window. "Ennis's."

He steered into traffic. "How long you staying there?"

"Indefinitely."

I did *not* feel like talking about this.

But Bryan didn't care.

"You *really* giving her the house?" he asked.

"Yeah."

I'd given the now-ex everything. Everything she'd wanted, that was, which turned out to be a lot.

What the hell. The woman deserved it.

She'd put up with two years of my bullshit. When it came down to it, she actually deserved a fucking award.

My girl—well, now my ex-girl—had started out a basic groupie. But she was different. Beautiful, witty. All eyes on her when she entered a room. I fell for her. Hard.

But that didn't keep my dick in my pants. No, I ruined it by continuing to be the man-whore I'd always been. Love didn't have anything to do with it.

She'd put up with it. And me. For a while, anyway.

One day I came home from tour a day early and found her in the company of another guy, some dude she'd met at one of my concerts. I turned right around and left for Ennis's.

I wasn't even mad. Who could blame her?

Bryan pulled up in front of Ennis's house. "Mind if I come in? I need to talk to you guys."

I kind of wanted to take a shower and wash the jail off me. "Yeah, sure. I'm tired, though."

"Don't worry. Won't take long."

"Ennis!" I hollered when we entered the house.

"Christ, dude. I'm right here," he said, raising an arm and waving from in front of the TV, where he was watching basketball.

Bryan walked around one of the three sofas filling Ennis's living room and took a seat. "Hey, got a minute to talk?"

Ennis grabbed the remote and turned the TV off. "Sure, Bry. What's up?"

They waited for me to join them, which I reluctantly did. I was quickly running out of what I called *socializing energy*. I wanted to be alone. Now.

"You probably know your buddy here spent last night in the big house."

Ennis's head whipped in my direction. "Again? Jesus, Stone. I wondered where you were. Figured you were shacking up with some chick."

'If you can't get laid, then get in a fight' was what my father had always said.

I spread my arms across the sofa back. "Apparently, I got into it with the wrong person this time."

Whatever. When you could fill a stadium like Dirty Bandit did, no one gave a shit what you did off the clock. As long as they could make money off you, you were golden.

And once the money dried up? Well, that was a different story. But that wasn't the case for us. We were going strong.

"Yeah, Stone punched out someone from the record label."

I wouldn't really say I *punched*—

"You did *what?*" Ennis roared. "Jesus, Stone. Are you a fucking idiot? Are you trying to ruin it for all of us?"

"You guys need to calm down—" I started to say. Fuckers were giving me a headache.

Ennis jumped to his feet. "So help me, Stone. If there's blowback from this—"

"Guys!" Bryan said in a raised voice. "No sense arguing. The label has been in touch with me. That's what I needed to talk to you about. We have to loop Hugh in on this, but they basically said if you all don't get it together, they're going to revisit the *out* clause in your contract."

I wasn't expecting that.

"And what the fuck did *I* do?" Ennis shouted. "I'm not the one making this band look like a bunch of hot-headed assholes."

Bryan held his hands up like a *stop* sign. "Wait a minute here. Your cocaine bust last year did not reflect well on Dirty Bandit, in case you forgot, Ennis."

My bandmate raked his fingers through the long hair falling over his eyes, then pulled a rubber band off his wrist and yanked it all into a ponytail.

I gave him endless shit about that. Only douchebag guys wore ponytails.

"What are we supposed to do?" I asked.

Bryan looked from one of us to the other. "I've

hired a public relations firm. We have our first meeting with them tomorrow. Here."

You could have heard a pin drop. At least until Ennis erupted.

"That's bullshit, Bryan. We don't need some stupid PR firm that's going to have us do cheesy good deeds to show the world Dirty Bandit isn't a bunch of druggies who love to fight."

"Really? How do you propose we change public opinion and make the label happy? At least happy enough to keep your world tour scheduled?"

Had he just mentioned something about our tour?

They had threatened to pull the world tour?

Bryan stood to leave. "Meeting's here at ten a.m. I'll call Hugh on my way home."

And he was gone.

Ennis and I sat looking at each other, speechless. I'd known him since I was about twelve, and this was a first.

"Stone, you know this is your fault," Ennis spat at me.

Wow. Just wow.

I headed for the French doors that led to the patio. The sun was glistening on the pool, and I needed nothing more than a dip to cool myself off. It might have been Ennis's house, but I sure as hell made myself at home.

I turned back to him. "Yeah. It's all *my* fault. *I* put that coke in your pocket, which you stupidly tried to take through airport security, right? At least I can say I was drunk when I fucked up. What's your excuse?"

I slammed the door behind me to drown out whatever lame answer he had for me. I dropped my T-shirt, jeans, and boxers on the patio deck and dove into the heated pool, the water rushing by, washing away as much of my shit day as it could.

## 6

CORAL

"You still have your scrubs on."

My BFF Nikki looked down at her shapeless blue-green clothing and nodded as she settled into the booth opposite me. "Yeah. I didn't have time to change. I got a little *hung up*," she said with a wink.

Sounded like there was a story. Nikki always had a story.

And she always wore scrubs. She swore they attracted guys like nobody's business.

The server dropped off our margaritas, Nikki's with salt and mine without. Both on the rocks.

"Cheers," I said, clinking my glass against hers. I took one, tiny delicious sip. I needed to make this cocktail last. Tomorrow was a big day, and I figured I'd be up late preparing.

To dazzle my arch nemeses. The thought made the taste of the margarita spoil on my tongue for a moment.

Nikki set her glass down after licking off a blob of salt from the rim. "Okay. Before I tell you about my day, tell me why you look so tired."

Was it that obvious?

I sighed. I probably shouldn't have been drinking at all if I looked *that* bad.

"I'm going through a stressful bout at work."

Wait until she heard.

She frowned. "Really? I thought you loved your job and your boss."

Ugh. I was going to have to tell her the whole, ugly story. I'd never shared it with anyone I'd met on this side of it.

"I do. I love my job. I love my boss. I'm freaking lucky to have them both. But, things are getting… complicated."

She leaned forward, excited. "What? Tell me!"

I looked around to check for privacy and lowered my voice. "We just signed Dirty Bandit."

"*Dirty Bandit?*" she screeched.

I sunk lower in our booth and looked around to see what kind of attention we'd attracted.

Fortunately, only a couple people had looked our way before going back to their own business.

"You can't tell anyone, Nikki. Promise me."

She crossed her heart and held up her hand, which meant she was totally going to tell everyone she knew.

"First off, that's awesome. But more importantly, when can I meet them?" she asked in a conspiratorial whisper, rubbing her hands together.

*Now* she was keeping her voice down.

"Don't ask me that."

She raised her hands in surrender. "So what's so bad about working with the world's biggest rock band?"

"They're dicks. Plain and simple."

The past played through my head like an old movie: the ordeal of the girls' locker room, the cruel, dismissive snickers. The writing on my locker, the pointing in the lunchroom. The invitations that never came.

She shrugged. "Huh? I mean, yeah. They're rock stars. Being dicks is inevitable—"

"I grew up with the guys, Nikki. I know them."

Her eyes grew wide. "No fucking way."

I nodded. "Until I went to college, I was a chubby geek, and certain people at school... ya know, weren't very nice to me and my small crew of friends. The usual bullshit. So yeah, my high school years were rather unhappy."

"Huh? *You?*" Nikki looked at me like I had two heads.

"Yeah. Me."

"Bu... but you're so pretty now. And slim. And hot. And successful."

It was amazing how quickly accomplishments could be forgotten. And lovely that *successful* was the last word she'd used to describe me.

"Thank you, Nikki. That's very nice of you to say. But the high school years were not kind to me. And neither were Ennis, Stone, or Hugh of Dirty Bandit."

"Oh my god. It's so weird to hear you say their names. As if they grew up around the corner from you."

They had. And after all these years, I didn't particularly like saying their names. Or even thinking about them. And certainly not listening to their music.

"What did they do to you?" she asked quietly.

I hesitated. But Nikki had been my best friend since I'd moved to Santa Monica two years before. I could tell her anything. She'd never think less of me.

"They... used to laugh and point. Crap like that. All the Populars did. But they were part of the group. They were basically in charge of it."

She looked impressed. "They were popular in high school? I always thought struggling musicians were outcast types. You know, slinking around in the corners of high school, unnoticed and unappreciated. Sneaking cigarettes in the bathroom. That sort of thing."

I wrapped my arms around myself, fighting off a sudden shiver.

"Christ, Coral," Nikki said, reaching for my hand. "That's terrible. Wow. I'm so sorry, honey. What assholes. I'll never listen to them again. And I never would have believed you were a 'fish out of water,' " she added with air quotes.

*Fish out of water.* That was the perfect way to put it. Some kids floated through adolescence like it was made for them. Others of us struggled every day, clawing through the muck to survive a little longer until it was over. Or mostly over.

I'd thought that shit was behind me. Maybe it was. But not far enough.

"Now it makes sense why you wouldn't want to work with them. I wouldn't want to, either. Have you told your boss?"

I swirled the ice in my glass and nodded. "I tried to."

We each watched the ice melting in our glasses, lost in thought.

Nikki drummed her fingers on the table. "Well, I've never told you about *my* childhood."

Oh my god. She hadn't.

"You're right. I never realized that. And now that I think of it, neither of us talks about our pasts. Funny, isn't it?"

I guess I'd not asked about hers because I didn't want her asking me about mine. I knew her as a fun-loving nurse who had nonstop stories about the hunky docs she worked with. She loved to go to the beach, go shopping, and drink cocktails.

We'd been on vacation in Maui together, where we'd done more of the same.

We just didn't talk about the sad times.

She continued. "My childhood wasn't pretty. My dad was constantly in and out of work. We'd get kicked out of apartments and have to spend the night in the car until another relative would take us in."

My god. She'd suffered in a way I couldn't imagine. It was terrible to be the butt of jokes in high school as I had been, but to not know where your next meal was coming from? That was another level of disadvantage altogether.

"I had no idea."

She held her head up. "I got picked on, too. Mostly for being dirty and smelly." She tossed back her long blonde hair.

It was almost impossible to imagine the beautiful, witty, and charismatic Nikki experiencing anything other than a life of privilege.

I squeezed her hand. "Well, look at us now."

She squeezed mine back. "Funny. I always knew there was something about you that connected the two of us. What are you gonna do?"

I shook my head. "I don't know. I have to meet with them tomorrow. Wait till they see me."

"Coral, they may not recognize or remember you."

I nodded. She may have been right. They wouldn't remember me. But *I* remembered *them*.

## 7

## CORAL

Any other time, I would have been psyched to visit someone's home in the glamorous, celebrity-filled Hollywood Hills. But this was not one of them.

I drove up one narrow, winding street after another, ogling the precariously suspended houses that looked as if they could slip right off their foundations at the slightest earthquake jolt.

This was where the guys from Dirty Bandit lived. Because, of course.

I should have insisted they come downtown for our meeting. I preferred the 'home court advantage' whenever possible, especially with clients I thought might be difficult. But Randall had told me their manager insisted I come to them, so I was shit out of luck.

When you were paying what they were, you got to pick your meeting locations.

I parked in front of a sprawling Spanish-style home covered in hot pink bougainvillea, and popped an Altoid in my mouth. I'd lain awake all night, and while I didn't fear falling asleep during my meeting, I was desperate to look at least a little alert. The sting of the strong mint gave me a modicum of confidence.

At least my breath wouldn't smell.

Teetering in the four-inch stilettos I wore only when I felt the need to potentially kick ass, I climbed the steep and numerous steps to the front door. I smoothed my hand over the ass of my clingy green Diane von Furstenberg wrap dress—the most expensive thing I'd ever bought—and flipped my blown-out hair back over my shoulders. I looked nice. I knew I did. Not like a supermodel, but I could hold my own.

Chanting my affirmation words *power* and *confidence*, I pressed the doorbell.

And waited.

Then waited some more.

I pressed it again.

When the door finally flew open, a guy I didn't recognize extended his hand.

I hadn't expected that. I figured they'd look the same as they did when we were seventeen. But I didn't look like that any longer, so why would they?

"I'm Hugh. Why don't you come in?"

Holy shit. Last time I'd seen Hugh, he'd been gangly and pasty, his face dotted with zits. And, I was pretty sure he'd been throwing a wadded-up straw wrapper at me in the senior lunchroom.

Lucky for him, his school years had safely ensconced him with the Populars by virtue of his association with the gorgeous Stone and the gregarious Ennis. Otherwise, he'd been a quiet, shy, easy-to-overlook kid.

But no more.

While he was still tall and slender, his once-narrow shoulders had broadened, shaped by the smooth muscles of someone who took pride in keeping fit but didn't go overboard with weights.

His previously bad complexion was smooth and lightly tanned, sprinkled with the scruff of a couple days of missed shaving.

But what really took me by surprise was his shaved head and neck tattoo, turning his boyish, sweet face into something slightly badass. If that were even possible. And holy crap, he was hot. Even the tiny creases in the corners of his eyes were perfection.

I cleared my throat.

*Power. Confidence.*

"Hi, Hugh. I'm Coral."

A small man pushing his glasses up on his nose came rushing past Hugh, hand extended. "Hi Coral, I'm Bryan, Dirty Bandit's manager. Thank you for coming up to the Hills. I hope you found the place okay. Your boss volunteered you for the trek so we wouldn't have to come downtown."

*Thanks*, Randall.

I entered a foyer perfectly in keeping with the house's Spanish style architecture and stepped into a living room expanse of white stucco walls, terra cotta tile, and exposed ceiling beams. Across the room, on the other side of open French doors, was a glittering swimming pool.

Utterly charming and utterly breathtaking. And a far cry from my apartment's view right into my neighbor's messy kitchen.

"This way, Coral," Bryan said, gesturing toward the sunken living room.

When I got closer, I recognized Stone and Ennis, and for a moment, I thought I might pass out. I gripped the back of a cushy chair just in case I started to go down. It would be only seconds now until they figured out who I was and laughed my ass right out of there.

But I kept my head up, smiled like I owned the place, and jumped in before anyone else could. "Bryan, before we start, do you think I could have some water?" I asked.

"Sure thing. And Coral, I'd like you to meet Stone and Ennis," he said, pointing in their direction.

I waited for even a slight flicker of recognition on their faces, which I was sure would turn to disgust when they remembered me as the awkward dork of

Perry High. But when they stood to greet me, I saw nothing more than the slightly-forced, polite smiles of people in a meeting when they'd rather be elsewhere.

Huh.

They extended their hands and Stone headed for the kitchen, walking in loose, low-slung jeans with the swagger of someone who'd been destined for great things since birth and had never had a doubt about where he was going.

Apparently, he was the worst of the lot in terms of bad behavior, having just spent a night in county jail for fighting. Or so I'd just read in one of those celebrity gossip tabloids.

He didn't look that different from high school. His blond hair had darkened a little and his arms were covered in sleeve tattoos, but he had the same chiseled jaw made all the more sexy by the passage of a few years.

Was it possible he was more handsome than ever?

Life was so not fair.

"Make yourself at home, Coral," the other band member, Ennis said, gesturing toward one of the room's huge leather club chairs.

He waited for me to sit and grabbed his own place on the sofa. Facing him, I realized how different he was from the round-faced boy I remembered from high school. He was now deliciously mature with even a little gray around the temples, the rest of his hair pulled back into a small ponytail. And the dimples. He still had the damn dimples.

I'd already been nervous, but my unease was now nuclear. I hadn't counted on them being so goddamn hot. And they were looking at me. All of me.

"You live around here?" Ennis asked as Stone returned with my water.

Yeah, PR hacks live in the Hollywood Hills. Talk about being out of touch with reality.

"Santa Monica." I left out the part about my shitty view, taking a sip of water and looking around. "Great house. All you guys live here?" I asked.

He closed his eyes and laughed, the dimples popping into view. "No. This is *my* house. Stone's staying here since his recent break up, and Hugh lives down the street.

Walking distance of each other, just as when they were kids.

Their smug confidence permeated the room, chafing me without mercy. What if I took them down? They needed me right now, which gave me the perfect opportunity to fuck them up.

That would be some serious revenge.

It would also be vindictive and immature, not to mention self-destructive. I had way more to lose than they did, I supposed, like my job, my future, my home…

"Where shall we begin, gentlemen?" I asked, leaning back in my chair, slowly crossing my legs.

Could I channel Sharon Stone in *Basic Instinct*, just without the crotch shot?

Either way, I got their attention. The three band members looked at each other then back at me.

It was Bryan who broke the silence by clearing his throat. "Dirty Bandit has been getting some bad press lately, as you may know, Coral. It's impacting our music sales. And we all know what that means." He pressed his lips together and looked at the guys.

If he was expecting them to jump in and elaborate on their fuck-ups, well, they hadn't gotten the memo.

They just glared at him like recalcitrant little punks in trouble with the school principal.

That aside, it was dawning on me how little I knew about the music industry, which was kind of amazing for someone who'd grown up in LA. But I wasn't about to let on. I just nodded in concern. Like a quiet, understanding therapist.

But Stone, arms across the back of the sofa where he sat in a serious *manspread*, decided not to let Bryan get the last word. "He's afraid his paycheck's gonna dry up," he said with a sneer.

Anger flashed across Bryan's face. "What Stone is saying, Coral, is that everyone's paycheck is in danger when you displease your record label. I've seen it before. Remember when the band Disciple faded into oblivion?" He glared back at the guys.

I vaguely remembered them, but I was pretty out of

the loop on rock music. I hoped I could keep it that way.

"They *faded*, Bryan, because their music sucked—" Stone started to say.

Bryan held his hand up. "No. They disappeared because they couldn't stay out of trouble. Everywhere they went they destroyed hotel rooms, got arrested for drugs, and the final straw was when one of them impregnated another band member's wife."

It blew my mind that people could live with such impunity. But I guess there was a price to pay—a steep one in the case of Disciple—and that you only got away with crap like that for so long.

"Christ, Bryan, we're not *that* bad," Ennis said, rolling his eyes.

"Really? Your coke bust last year was no big deal, huh? And Stone's two arrests this year were just for the fun of sleeping in a jail cell?"

Jesus. What was I getting into? Did Randall know all this shit? I mean, I was good at PR, but I didn't know about cleaning up disasters like this.

Maybe these guys weren't the blessed-by-the-gods men I'd thought they were.

Bryan, apparently not done scolding the guys, turned to Hugh. "And didn't you punch a photographer a few months ago?"

Holy shit. Was it too late to turn and run? Could I handle this, and these assholes?

Bryan turned back to me, satisfied he'd made a strong case. "Now you see why we need you."

8

---

ENNIS

If Bryan didn't stop talking to us like we were bad little kids, I was going to lose It. Seriously. I could only take so much of his scolding.

And he was making us look like major douchebags in front of the hot PR girl. What was her name again? Carol? Carla?

It didn't matter. She wouldn't be around long enough for us to need to know her name.

But damn if she didn't look familiar. I couldn't place her, but the long red hair and nice tits got my motor revving. And my dick stirring.

Redheads did that to me.

And that fucking green dress she wore. On one

hand, it had that uptight librarian vibe with its pointy collar and long sleeves. But the low neckline and clingy fabric blasted its sex quotient so far off the charts I could barely see straight.

I tried to focus on something else in the room. It didn't work.

The way she'd crossed her legs showed just enough of her lightly tanned knees, and the heels she was wearing—well, it was clear she didn't plan to do much walking.

Just my type. I figured I must have fucked her at some point, and that was why she was familiar. It seemed I'd fucked nearly every beautiful woman in LA, anyway. Had I met her at a show? Or maybe chatted her up at some party?

Either way, I wouldn't mind getting her naked again. Especially if she kept those shoes on.

I could see Stone felt the same way. He'd barely moved his gaze from her shapely legs the whole time she'd been sitting there. Hugh, on the other hand, was probably enticed as well. But he was way more discreet than we were.

The bastard.

In fact, Stone was so mesmerized, I had to give him an accidental kick to the shin to bring his attention back to the room.

Bryan's phone buzzed, and he looked at the screen. "Sorry guys, Coral, I have to take this."

*Coral.* That was her name.

He scurried off to the backyard, leaving the hot PR girl with us.

Fuck, I wondered if she'd be game…

*Down boy. Not the right time.*

Stone popped to his feet and began to pace, walking close enough to Coral to brush her chair, like an animal in the wild asserting his dominance.

Coral, to her credit, pretended not to notice and kept her attention trained on Hugh and me.

"We don't need a fucking PR person," Stone growled, his shoulders hunched and his fists tight.

Still, she showed no reaction. I had to hand it to her.

He looked at her hard. "We are under a lot of pressure. Something you'd never understand."

Here comes dick Stone. Sometimes you got nice Stone. But today was not that day.

She finally looked up at him where he loomed over her.

"You're right," she said. "I have no idea of the stresses you face."

Stone nodded, carrying on. "We're under an incredible amount of pressure. Each album has to be better than the last, and each tour has to outsell the last. Add to that, every fucking band out there wants our position as number one. It's insane," he said, running his hands through his hair as he loped across the long room and back.

A sudden movement caught everyone's eye, and we

turned to see Bryan rush back into the house, his face red.

"I knew this would happen," he growled, his hands in fists. "You guys couldn't be happy with all the good fortune that's come your way. You just had to fuck it up."

What the fuck?

He chewed on a thumbnail and stared out the window at the mountains.

"Jesus, Bryan. We love you, too," Stone said flippantly.

Hugh leaned forward in his seat, frowning. "What the hell happened, Bryan? What's going on?"

Stone stopped pacing.

Bryan shook his head slowly. "That was the record label. They're about to pull the plug."

I watched Coral's head snap back as the room erupted into a litany of *that's bullshit, fuck those assholes,* and other protests against the insults visited on us.

"Let them dump us, Bryan. We'll just go to another label," I said.

"It's not that easy, Ennis, and you know it," he snapped. "They'll say you're a *bad bet.*"

"I don't see how filling a stadium to capacity for a show is a *bad bet.* Are they fucking idiots?" Stone shouted. "We don't need them," he said, throwing his arms in the air.

Then he picked up a glass and flung a glass across

the room, where it shattered on the wall—*my* wall—the liquid inside it splashing in every direction.

"Don't throw shit in my house, Stone," I hollered.

Asshole was going to clean that up later.

"Shut up. Both of you. Just shut up," Hugh said quietly, rubbing his hand over his bald head.

In fact, he said it so quietly that everyone in the room actually did shut up.

He turned to Coral, who had jumped to her feet, her sky-high heels clicking across my tile floor. Her green dress swung back and forth just above her knees, the silky fabric skimming her round bottom.

She had our attention now.

## 9

# ENNIS

Coral waved some newspaper clipping around in her hand, moving it too fast for me to read. But I knew it had to be bad news.

She turned to face us and looked from one to the other to ensure we were listening.

"I can help you," she said simply.

The room was silent.

She continued. "I can help you keep your contract with the record label. I can help you improve your reputation. I can help you get publicity that will make you the kind of band that people admire for many things, and not just your music."

Stone, perpetually unable to keep his mouth shut,

crossed his arms, furious. "What you don't seem to understand is that all we want to be known for is our *music*. The other stuff is just fluff. It doesn't matter." He shook his head frantically.

Undeterred, Coral stood right in front of him, holding the newspaper clipping in his face. "See this photo here, of you about to punch some photographer?"

He glanced at it, then back at Coral.

She took a step closer and got in his face. "This is you being known for something *other* than music. You can't have it both ways. You do things like *this*. You are *known* for this. And you only get so many passes for *this* sort of thing. And if what your manager says is true, and we have no reason to believe it's not, then your passes have expired."

She was standing up to Stone. No one did that. Well, except for us guys.

And it worked. He actually sat back on the sofa, and shut his mouth.

But it wasn't going to work on me, I didn't care how hot she was or how many times I might have fucked her. When it came down to it, she didn't know shit about us or our business.

"You know, lady, I don't know who you think you are, but we don't need you to tell us how to conduct ourselves—" I started to say.

But before I could finish, she held her hand up like a

*stop* sign. "You're right. You don't need me to tell you anything."

She reached for her bag and headed for the door. "If you change your minds, you know where to reach me. I have a busy day ahead and don't need to waste anyone's time, especially people as busy as you guys."

She pulled the front door open and stepped into the bright LA sunshine. I could swear I saw a thong outline through the fabric of her dress.

"*Wait*." Bryan ran after her, pulling the door closed behind them.

"Well, you guys blew that one," Hugh said, sighing.

What the fuck?

"Dude. You've gotta be kidding," I said.

He held his hands up. "Look. Every big band does some of this PR shit. It makes a difference. I know it does. And if it means the label will keep us, then what's the goddamn harm? Seriously. Get over yourselves."

He looked from one of us to the other, the voice of reason in our trio. Ever since we were kids trying to make music, he'd been the one with the good head on his shoulders.

He continued. "You can't just give it a chance? See what the woman has to say. If her ideas suck, we'll send her packing. You know, if she hooks us up with a cheesy, star-studded *We are the World* concert, we'll say no thanks. But I, for one, would like to stay with our record label. I want to hear what she has to say."

I wasn't as convinced. I didn't need any distractions. I had a new album's worth of songs to write.

"Stone?" Hugh said, looking right at him.

He avoided his gaze then shrugged. "Yeah. Whatever, man. I don't think it will do a bit of good, but if you want to try it, I'll keep my damn mouth shut and go along."

Wow. Stone never acquiesced.

"Cool," Hugh said.

He turned to me. "Okay Ennis. Will you give it a shot? As a favor to me?"

A smile crept across my face. "A favor to you, huh? Did ya hear that Stone? Hugh is asking me for a favor."

Stone nodded, also smiling. "I heard. You gonna help the man out?"

Then, he burst out laughing so hard I couldn't help but join him, followed by Hugh.

"Yes, I'll do both you assholes a favor. I'm outvoted anyway, so what the hell?"

At the sound of our laughter, Bryan came back in the house with Coral on his heels.

She walked right up to us and our laughter subsided almost immediately. Her lips were pressed tightly together, and she was frowning.

Not what I'd expected of her.

"Look. You are on top of the world at this moment in time. Don't blow your ride."

She was cute when she was fired up. And her nipples were hard, a fact that wasn't lost on any of us.

Except for maybe Bryan who, as far as we all knew, was pretty much asexual.

"We were thinking the same thing," Hugh said. "We want to give you a shot."

Her eyes widened, and her head snapped back. "Oh. Really."

She sucked at disguising her surprise.

But a moment later she'd recovered. "Wonderful. Let's get started, then."

She returned to her seat, and re-crossed those gorgeous legs. Bryan set himself right next to her, standing and smiling like he'd discovered gold.

Maybe he had.

He wanted to keep his job just like the rest of us. And the man really didn't deserve the shit we sent his way. He'd stood by us through thick and thin, and always worked at least as hard as we did.

Coral continued. "We're going to clean up the Dirty Bandit image. You will do charity and volunteer work. You will donate part of your ticket sales. And I can assure you, it will all be painless. In fact, you may even enjoy it. Did you know one of the most philanthropic bands is Pearl Jam? And who doesn't love them?"

She seemed happy she could throw around the name of a big band. She didn't look like much of a rock 'n roll girl.

But Stone wasn't impressed. "Pearl Jam? Are you serious? Those guys are a bunch of old fuckers."

"They may be old, but they are respected, and have

had a long goddamn career. Much longer than most other bands."

Well. Coral had done her homework, and was taking no shit. I liked that in a woman.

Actually, I liked several things about this woman.

Hugh turned toward her. "Where do we start? And when do we start?"

10

## CORAL

"Let's get some things out in the open here," I said, mustering all my courage and staring down each of the guys. The idiots had no idea who I was. I was safe. The past was staying in the past.

My confidence exploded. I was on fire.

"I just need to be straight with you. Do you want a long-term career, or to burn out and be forgotten? I don't care either way. Personally, I have a stable job and there will always be some other band clawing their way to the top that wants our help. So, I have no stake in what you decide." I threw my hands up for dramatic effect.

Holy shit. Did I really just say that?

I gripped the arms of the leather chair where I sat so no one could see my hands trembling. I'd never been that forthright. Or rude.

I supposed it was never too late to become a ball buster.

But had I pulled it off? Had I earned a measure of respect from these spoiled, out-of-touch, man-children?

If only I could have been that ballsy in high school. Put these guys and their group in their place. Given the Populars the middle finger. It wouldn't have mattered if they kept ridiculing me. At least it would have shown a little self-respect.

And doesn't self-respect bring about respect?

But that was then, and I'd done the best I could at the time, which in the end was to just escape. I didn't know how else to change my situation except by exiting it as I had. And I was now worlds away from that awkward kid from Perry High.

Right?

At least, that's what I told myself. It helped with the bad memories.

Well, sometimes it helped. Today, not so much. When you were sitting right in front of your night-mare, what else would you expect?

And when I thought about it, the tirade I'd just thrown at the guys had been nothing short of the abso-lute truth. I couldn't give a shit whether they stayed on top or sank to the depths of obscurity. Seriously. I was fine either way, and I would continue to be fine either way. My boss would be disappointed if Dirty Bandit sent me packing, but in time there'd be another client right behind them, more eager and probably more deserving of the privileges that accompany rock star success.

So, I didn't have a thing to lose if they kicked me out. I'd go on about my day, dealing with other clients, going to my mani-pedi appointment, and seeing Nikki after work if she didn't have to take another shift at the hospital.

Of course, the band's manager would report back to my boss—they were friends from college or something like that, which is how our firm got the Dirty Bandit business. How would that go?

And speaking of Bryan, he was sitting directly across the room from me, wearing the oddest smirk.

Was he laughing at me? Or impressed with me?

Did I care?

Where had this confidence of mine been back in the day? Why had I let a little weight problem define me? I'd been so much more than a pair of chubby thighs. Of course, when you're living your tormented teen years, you have no idea what you have going for you. Not a freaking clue.

That was especially true for me.

It hadn't helped that my mother was not much better than the creeps at school. She'd sent me to Weight Watchers when I was only in sixth grade—

young enough that she'd had to sign a parental consent form, which she happily did.

She'd drop me off at the meetings at a nearby church, and I sat there alone, huddled in my folding chair, the only kid in a sea of adults who eyed me with sympathy as they talked about foods to avoid and healthy ones to cook.

As if I had any control over what I ate. My mother put a plate of food in front of me, and I was required to eat until was clean.

And as if that weren't bad enough, after the meetings, she'd take her sweet time picking me up. I'd be the last person waiting on the curb in front of the church, alone and in the dark.

At the time, I was neither afraid nor sad. I thought it was perfectly normal, having nothing else to compare it to. Years later, it finally pissed me off.

So yeah, I hadn't gotten much support from the home front.

In addition to Bryan's smirk, the guys had gone quiet after I'd given them a piece of my mind. They mostly just shifted in their seats, trying to look cool and tough but squirming under the truth I'd laid out.

Fuck them. If they blew their sweet ride, they deserved what they got.

But now that they were finally quiet, I could appreciate how damn beautiful each of them was.

And they were all three looking at me. Well, mostly my legs. But still.

So I was feeling pretty on top of the world.

That is, until Stone dropped a bomb. Of the nuclear proportion.

"Hey, Cora, where did you—"

"It's *Coral*. Her name is *Coral*," Bryan interrupted.

Stone side-eyed him and turned back to me. "Coral, where'd you go to high school? I could swear you look familiar."

Oh god oh god oh god.

No way could they remember me. No freaking way. My hair was now long and de-frizzed, I'd grown another inch or two taller, and I'd shrunk significantly in the waist department.

Oh yeah. I'd ditched the glasses and braces, too.

Had my true identity been discovered? Were they going to ridicule me again? Look down on me?

Make me feel fat, ugly, and not cool enough to hang out with them?

I could lie. Just make something up. They'd never know any better. Say I was from another state, even.

I could say I'd gone to Scottsdale High School in Scottsdale, Arizona.

Was there an actual Scottsdale High? I had no freaking idea. But it sounded good.

Ennis scratched his head. "You know, Stone, I was thinking she looked familiar, too," he said, squinting his eyes and studying me.

"No kidding, what a coincidence," Bryan said cheerfully, as if our being acquainted was destiny.

Me, not so much.

I'd just gone from my five seconds of power right back to the chubby nerd I was in high school. How the hell did that happen?

And just before I sank to the bottom of a crater of shame and self-pity, a surge of *fuck you* erupted in me. Screw those assholes.

"I went to Perry High School. Just like you guys did."

## 11

## CORAL

The guys' eyes widened, their thoughts running a mile a minute trying to recall exactly how our paths had crossed all those years ago. Clearly, they didn't remember me *that* well.

"No shit! Wow," Stone exclaimed. "Small world," he said excitedly, looking at Hugh and Ennis.

Still animated, he leaned forward. "Who'd you hang out with? Did you come to my parties?"

"Parties?" I asked. "Like when your band would practice in your parents' garage?"

Time for me to drop a little bomb of my own.

"Yes, exactly!" He looked over at the other guys.

"Can you believe this? We all went to high school together."

"Who'd you hang out with? I still can't quite place you. Were you part of Sully's group? Or Candy's?"

I wasn't sure who Sully or Candy were, but I was pretty sure they wouldn't have hung out with me back then.

Just like these guys wouldn't have.

I shook my head slowly, uncrossing, then re-crossing my legs. "I didn't hang out with any of those people. Or you guys, either."

Stone looked puzzled. "Really? Because we made a point of knowing all the pretty girls—"

"Stone, chill out," Hugh barked.

Wow. Didn't know Hugh was the barking type.

Hugh rubbed his hand over his head for about the tenth time. "Wait. I remember you now, Coral. Weren't you in Mrs. Siebert's English class?"

Oh my god. *He* was in Siebert's class, too? I'd completely forgotten he was one of the smart kids, like me.

I nodded slowly. "Yes, that's right. We were in English together, Hugh." If I remembered correctly, he was quiet, usually hanging out in the back of the room where the teacher wouldn't notice him.

Was this a good thing? Would it be easier to work with the guys now that we'd established some common ground?

Would I still be tormented by memories of my old teenage self?

As I was thinking about the different directions things could go, Stone jumped to his feet. "I know! You were the fat chick who sat with the other nerds in the senior lunchroom."

The room went silent as heat washed over my face and my stomach churned. Was it too late to just run out the door, head back to the office, and make up some bullshit story for my boss?

"Stone, sit down and shut up," Hugh said.

Stone looked around the room like a stupid little puppy who had no idea what he'd done wrong.

How was it that all I'd accomplished in the last ten years could be wiped away with one thoughtless remark? It was like he'd pushed me into a time machine and rolled back the clock.

My years of hard-earned confidence were rapidly unraveling. Who knew their hold had been so tenuous? I was no longer the self-assured woman sitting in a beautiful home in the Hollywood Hills, wearing a sexy designer dress and four-inch heels, talking to the leaders of the number one rock band in the world.

Nope. I was the chubby, insecure teenager *again*, confronted by a bunch of jerks who were shaming me to the depths of my soul.

I wanted to curl up into a little ball and roll away.

"Coral? Coral, are you okay? You look a little pale,"

Bryan said, walking toward me. "One of you guys go get more water, will you?"

That snapped me out of it. "I'm fine, thank you. I was just thinking back to those years in high school. So long ago."

I took a fresh glass of water from Hugh and gulped it down. The cool liquid calmed my stomach.

I looked directly at Stone and smiled. "Yeah, I was the fat kid. Nice of you to bring it up."

Dirty looks from the others in the room came at him.

*Take that.*

"Oh, well, I um…" he sputtered.

But I ran over his lame attempt to excuse himself. "Gentlemen. Right now, you're close to losing everything you have. There are a dozen other bands clamoring for your spot at the top of the charts. They are ready to *eat your lunch*, and from what I can tell, you are pretty much spoon feeding it to them. It's a shame to throw away what you've worked for. But if that's what you want to do…"

I shrugged helplessly, grabbed my bag, and stood to leave.

"*Wait.*" Hugh raised his hands like a *stop* sign. "Don't leave."

He looked at Stone and Ennis. "We need your help, hard as it is to admit. Good music is not enough. We need to clean up our act."

Finally. I had the fuckers.

12

12

---

HUGH

Wow. Just wow. It was inconceivable that the beautiful woman sitting across from us was the same chubby, frizzy-haired girl whose head I'd stared at the from the back of English class ten years ago.

'Course, it was hard to believe three punks from Perry High had made it to the heights of rock 'n roll fame, too.

So I guess we were all full of surprises.

We wrapped up our meeting. We'd tormented the poor woman long enough. Bryan was so relieved he looked like he might cry. He'd known full well that selling a PR firm to us was going to be an uphill battle, and it looked like he'd won.

For the moment, anyway. You never knew how Stone might fuck things up.

Speaking of Stone, I threw him the most discreet stink eye I could muster. I didn't want to make a scene—there'd already been enough of that—but I wanted him to know he was on my shit list.

He might be Dirty Bandit's lead singer, but he was also the one responsible for most of our problems. I was no angel, and neither was Ennis, but at least we kept our shit somewhat under control.

Coral, apparently having earned her stripes, was now being fawned on by Stone and Ennis. I had no doubt they each thought they might get into her panties, and they probably had a little competition going to see who could cock-block the other first. I wouldn't even be surprised if they placed a wager on who'd have a first go at her.

Yeah, they could be dicks that way.

So I decided to take control of the situation.

"Coral," I called to cut through the noise of the guys chatting her up.

The three of them turned my way.

"Why don't you let me take you to lunch?" I glanced at my watch. "My favorite restaurant on Sunset closes in half an hour. If we head out now, they'll seat us."

Coral frowned, then quickly corrected her expression. Had this woman taken acting lessons?

She glanced at her watch. "Um, sure. Okay."

I motioned toward the door. "Awesome. Let's roll then."

Stone and Ennis smiled slightly, realizing I'd outflanked them, and stepped aside.

They could suck it.

Minutes later, Coral and I settled into a sunny patio table and the waiter tipped an umbrella to provide her a little shade.

"Ah, much better," she said, smiling at him.

Now that I was close to her, I got a whiff of her light perfume. The scent was evasive—present one moment and gone the next, depending on how the breeze shifted.

She pushed her sunglasses up on her head and studied me. "So. Hugh Cairn. All these years later, our paths cross," she said after she'd taken a sip of the sangria the waiter had delivered.

I hadn't remembered how red her hair was. Glittering in the afternoon sun, it tumbled in waves over her shoulders and down the front of her green dress.

Goddamn, she was gorgeous.

I sat back in my chair and just gawked. I couldn't help it.

"Crazy, isn't it?" I muttered, wondering if she remembered how we guys were such shits to her and her posse.

*Of course* she remembered. No one forgets things like that.

And yet, here she was, being gracious as all get

out. 'Course, she really had no choice. We were most likely paying her firm a princely amount. People would put up with a lot of shit for the right amount of money.

She leaned closer after looking around at the other diners. "I hadn't anticipated people staring like this. Does it happen all the time?"

I shrugged. I was so used to it I barely noticed. It had been hard at first, though, having people always in your business.

But Bryan had told us this was how it would be. And we'd decided it was worth it.

Although sometimes I wasn't sure.

Something glinted from the street.

Shit.

"What was that? A photographer?" she asked quietly.

"Yup. They're around a lot. It's weird. Why are people interested in me? I'm boring as hell."

With that, Coral dropped her head back and laughed out loud.

I didn't remember her doing that in high school, just like I didn't remember her glowing hair. But then, I'd had my head so far up my ass those days, it was amazing I'd even graduated, regardless of the 'smart kid' classes they'd thrown me in.

"You know," she started, "it is really interesting how people are fascinated with celebrities. Here you are, just having some lunch, and someone wants a photo of you. You're not performing music or running around naked. You're just sitting here."

Another flash.

I ignored it. But Coral didn't.

"Is that bothering you, Hugh? I can go to talk to him."

I shook my head and leaned closer for privacy, getting another whiff of her lovely perfume. "Don't. It will only backfire. Taking action—well, inappropriate action—is what has gotten us into so much trouble. We really have no rights in these situations unless someone has trespassed onto our property."

"I suppose."

"Although," I said, craning my neck around the other late-lunch diners, "I've seen that particular guy before. He's a real weasel, always looking to make trouble."

She reached into her purse and retrieved her phone. "Do me a favor. Chill out here. I'm going to pretend to head to the ladies' room, but I'm going to go around the side of the restaurant and snap a photo of him. Just so we have it."

I had no idea why the hell she'd want a photo of a pain in the ass paparazzi, but hey, she could do whatever the hell she wanted.

"I'll be here," I said, admiring her as she stood.

As she walked away, I couldn't help but notice that the cadence of her walk made her ass jiggle just the tiniest bit.

My kryptonite. A nice ass.

13

HUGH

It was so uncanny, running into Coral after all these years. Even though I couldn't say I really knew her aside from simply recognizing her, there was some comfort in knowing we had a few things in common.

And it didn't hurt that she was bewitchingly striking.

Speaking of which, how did a woman go from being, well... how Coral was in high school, to a shapely, statuesque beauty who turned heads when she walked across a room?

Like she was doing just then, hustling back to our table to enjoy her smoked salmon salad.

"I got a pic of him," she said breathlessly, oblivious to the heads turning in her direction.

She dove into her salad. "I'm glad you suggested lunch. To be honest, I was starving."

I loved a woman with an appetite.

And now it was time to call out the elephant in the room.

"I'm sorry about what Stone said earlier. He can be such a douchebag."

She pressed her lips together while she considered my words, then shrugged. "Well, he was right. I was… pretty awkward back then." She returned to her salad, avoiding my gaze.

But that wasn't the end of my apology. I knew that girls like her in high school were not treated well. At all.

"I… had a lot of shit going on at home when I was a kid. It wasn't pretty."

As soon as I said it, I regretted it. What a lame fucking excuse. Use a crappy family situation as the reason for being unkind. But it got her attention.

She set down her fork. "Really?"

Shit. I hated discussing this stuff. But if we were going to work together, I needed to clear the air.

And maybe my conscience, as well.

"Yeah. It was a fucked-up situation. To this day, I don't have anything to do with my father or mother."

She nodded slowly. "I'm sorry to hear that."

"Yeah. My dad was a bastard, and my mom just

went along so he wouldn't turn on her. As a result, I wasn't the nicest person back then. Probably still not the nicest person."

Ah, regrets.

I could swear Coral's eyes were teary.

"So here's to getting the hell out of Dodge," I said, raising my glass.

Unfortunately, my getting out of Dodge meant I'd not seen my long-suffering mother in years. Last time I'd tried to send her money, she'd begged me not to. Said my dad would take it out on her if he ever found it.

Broke my fucking heart.

We clinked glasses. "Sometimes I feel badly about escaping. You know what I mean?"

Her eyes widened. "Oh my god, I do too. I wondered if I was the only person who felt that way."

Another thing we had in common. "Maybe the guilt never goes away."

"Well, I guess adulthood is all about reinventing yourself. There's no shame in leaving the past behind. At least that's what I tell myself," she said.

"Right? I mean, why should we feel badly about leaving bad shit behind?" I shook my head.

Time for a lighter topic.

"So, Coral, what other bands have you guys worked with?"

She dabbed the corners of her mouth with a napkin, I think in part to hide that she was furiously blushing.

What was up with that?

"I have to come clean with you, Hugh."

She looked tortured. Which I loved.

"You're our first band. I'm supposed to keep that quiet, but since you asked, I'm not about to lie."

I dropped my head back and laughed. "Shit, Coral, I have no problem with that. In fact, I'm glad you haven't worked with any other bands. That means you'll have some fresh ideas for us."

She nodded with enthusiasm and glanced at her watch. "I can't wait to get started. In fact, I better get back to the office before my boss thinks you guys kidnapped me."

Might not be a bad idea…

We wandered to the front of the restaurant, neither of us in a hurry to leave. While we waited for the valet to bring each of our cars around, I turned to Coral.

"Hey, about your not having worked with any other bands…"

Her face dropped. "I should not have told you that. Please don't tell Bryan. I don't know what my boss told him."

I moved a little closer as a sort of test. Her eyes remained wide open.

So I picked up a strand of her hair, and ran it through my fingers. It was silky and warm from the sun. I would have liked to run all my fingers through it, but that would surely be a step too far.

"I'll tell ya what, Coral."

"Yeah?" she said, looking up at me, her eyes wide.

And now I was getting a hard-on, dammit.

"Your secret is safe with me."

"Oh good. Thank you," she said, smiling broadly.

"In exchange for… a little kiss."

She took a step back and wrinkled her nose. "*What?*"

I wasn't giving up so easily.

"I think you heard me. I'd like a kiss. In exchange, I promise not to divulge your secret."

The valet pulled my car up, and she looked around nervously for hers.

Which had not arrived yet.

"Well, um, I don't think—"

I leaned down, and with my hand on the back of her neck, pressed my lips to hers before she could finish.

At first, she tensed, her hands flying to my torso as if to push me away. But as I lightly brushed her lips with my own, she actually moved toward me, her hands relaxing on my chest.

And damn if she didn't taste sweet, just like I knew she would.

I watched her eyes flutter closed, and the slightest moan sneaked out of her throat. God, she was delicious. And I wanted more.

Hopefully, there'd be time for that, another day.

"Well," I said, abruptly pulling back from her. "Your secret's safe now, isn't it?"

With her lips slightly parted, she stood, looking at

me for a moment, then tossed her hair back over her shoulders.

"Oh. Right. Well, thanks."

She cleared her throat and smoothed her dress.

It was fucking adorable.

Her car had arrived, and I led her to the driver's side door, inching the valet guy out of the way, and holding her hand as she lowered herself into her Prius.

"Looking forward to our next meeting," I said, closing her car door and leaning in the window.

"Yeah, me, too," she said, jamming her car into gear.

I was watching her drive off into LA traffic until her Prius was out of sight when my phone buzzed with a text.

It was Ennis.

*where are you? did you run off with her?*

Not a bad idea.

## CORAL

I kicked my shoes off and buried my head in my hands as soon as I closed my office door.

What a freaking day.

Hugh.

Hugh Cairn.

I wracked my brain for a visual of Mrs. Siebert's English class. I hadn't paid much attention to the back-of-the-class kids, just like they probably hadn't paid much attention to me.

I hadn't ever thought about it, but where you sat in class said a lot about you when you were in high school. Unless the teacher assigned seats, like alpha-betical order or something, everyone gravitated toward their friends or other kids with similar interests.

You weren't likely to see the brainy kids voluntarily sit next to the stoners, let's put it that way.

But the little I remembered was that I'd written him off as just another pothead, even if he were one of the Populars, content to sit in the back of class, take tests when he had to, and put forth little other effort.

Maybe my own assumptions back then were no better than their putting me into the 'chubby nerd' category. Were we all guilty of that?

Were we still doing it now?

My office door flew open. No knock. I knew who it was without even looking up.

"Hi, Lucy."

The office troublemaker waltzed in uninvited, the topknot in her hair so tight it pulled the skin of her face back.

It looked painful.

She was the kind of person who, if we were still in high school, would never have spoken to me.

"Coral. Heard you got the Dirty Bandit account." She puckered her glossy lips together and narrowed her eyes.

Never a good sign.

"Yeah, I guess so."

She helped herself to a seat.

"You *guess* so? That's all you can say about working with the world's number one rock band?"

Guess I wouldn't tell her one of them had kissed me.

"Lucy, I have a lot of work to do. Is there something I can help you with?"

She got up in a huff, her freakishly narrow hips encased in the world's tightest pencil skirt.

"I should have gotten that account," she snarled.

Damn. If I had anything to say about it, she could totally have it.

But I didn't.

"Did you share your concerns with Randall?" I asked her, running a finger over my lips where Hugh had just kissed me.

Shit. Was I going to be able to get any work done today? I could still smell his scent—plain soap, nothing fancy.

"Yeah. But you're his pet. Everyone knows you're his pet. That's why you get the best clients—"

I pushed myself to my feet. I really didn't have the energy for any more drama, especially since Lucy pulled a temper tantrum like this at least once a month.

"Lucy, that's not true, and you know it."

She scowled at me one last time and stormed out of my office.

The truth was, if Randall had a pet, it probably *would* be me, but not for any frivolous reason. I worked my ass off for him and his firm, to the extent that I had little social life and absolutely no love life.

The man rewarded dedication. That's all there was to it.

Lucy didn't fall into that category with all her complaining, shitty attitude, and missed deadlines.

But that still didn't mean I was pleased to be working with Dirty Bandit, Hugh's sexy kiss notwithstanding. They were going to be a pain in the ass of epic proportion. I just knew it.

I had no doubt they were still the dicks they'd been in high school. People only changed so much, regardless of how they looked on the outside.

I settled into my chair and scrolled through all the emails I'd missed. But my thoughts kept wandering back to lunch.

Dammit.

Hugh—hell, all those guys—probably kissed every decent-looking woman who crossed their paths. He had no interest in me. He was just looking to embarrass me or otherwise exert control because he knew as soon as our work got underway, I'd be driving things.

Hopefully.

But his lips sure had been nice on mine—

"Coral!" Randall chirped, poking his head through my doorway and scaring the shit out of me.

"How'd everything go?"

I gestured for him to take a seat, which was weird because he was the boss and could sit anywhere he wanted. "Randall, come on in," I said, clearing my desk of scattered papers as a sign of respect.

He rubbed his hands together. "Bryan, Dirty Bandit's manager called me just a few minutes ago."

Oh shit, oh shit, oh shit.

God, that man didn't waste any time. I knew he'd eventually report back to Randall what a rude bitch I'd been, but I thought he'd at least wait a day or two. I looked around my office with a quick glance, sizing up how much I could take with me in case Randall was kicking my ass out.

"Oh, he called. Great." I tried to sound enthusiastic, but my words were flat. Dull. Like I was going to feel after Randall fired me.

I even slipped my shoes back on in preparation for a quick exit.

Lucy would be happy to see me gone, that was for sure. Maybe she could even have the Dirty Bandit account, if they hadn't fired the firm altogether.

Wonder if Hugh would try to kiss her, too…?

Randall nodded. "Sounded like the meeting was very interesting." He looked at me expectantly.

But since I didn't know what he wanted to hear, and figured it wouldn't make a difference anyway, I just nodded.

"Wh… what were Bryan's impressions?" I croaked.

I'd make him blink first. That way I'd know how to respond.

"He said…"

Why was he hesitating? Just fucking get it over with.

"...he said you were brilliant. You had the guys eating out of your hand."

Well, damn. Were there empty boxes in the mail-room? Because I could load my shit in one and be out the door in minutes. Although I might need two boxes, if I were to claim the spider plant I'd nursed back from death. I probably didn't need all the mugs I'd brought, which everyone in the office was using now, anyway.

"Coral? Coral, are you listening?"

I stood to gather my stuff.

"Yes, Randall, I'm listening." I grabbed my sneakers from under the desk and crammed them in my tote bag.

"Coral, Bryan thought you were awesome."

I couldn't find my favorite coffee cup. But I could always get another.

*Wait.*

Had he said Bryan *liked* me? Or something like that?

"Sorry, Randall. What did you say?"

His brow was furrowed. I'm sure letting me go was not easy for him. I was one of his first employees.

"Coral, please sit down. This is an important conversation."

I fell back into my chair, purse and tote bag on my lap.

"Apparently you did a great job of convincing them of the firm's expertise. Bryan is really excited about working with you. And, all of us, really."

Huh? Randall was happy?

I still had a job?

Holy shit.

I tossed my things on the floor next to my desk. "Bryan said it was a good meeting?" I asked unsteadily.

He beamed. "Said you handled the guys like a pro. Showed them who was boss." He slammed his hands on my desk and pushed himself up to go. But before he did, he turned around.

"I knew you'd knock it out of the park, kiddo," he said with a wink.

And pulled my door closed behind him.

Holyfuckingshit.

I still had a job.

And even better, both the client and my boss were happy with me.

And I'd just been kissed by a big-ass rock star.

## 15

## CORAL

"You. Are. Such. A. Ho," Nikki screamed, slapping my arm and nearly knocking me off my barstool.

I wiped the beer off my arm that she'd spilled. "Take it easy, would you? And pipe down."

I looked around to see if anyone had heard us.

"Fine," she said, whispering. "You fucking kissed Hugh Cairn. That is even more amazing than the story I have to tell."

I could just imagine her 'amazing story.' I'd bet a thousand dollars it had something to do with hot doctors and hospital supply closets.

She shimmied her shoulders and closed her eyes, as

if *she* were kissing Hugh. "Okay. Now tell me. What was it like?"

I'd spent nearly every moment since Hugh's kiss thinking about it, but now that the initial shock had worn off, I had to say it was pretty damn sexy.

I just hoped that creepy photographer had been nowhere in the vicinity.

Putting my head closer to Nikki, I spoke quietly. "I liked it, Nikki. And what was especially hot was that I didn't expect it. He just did it. Like he was *taking* something."

Her eyes widened. "Oh my god. I know exactly what you mean. Like when they kind of dominate you, or something?"

She grinned maniacally.

Dominate. I'd never considered that. What accomplished, strong woman wanted to be dominated?

And yet, it was so freaking delicious how he'd put his hand on the back of my neck and just kissed me like I had no say in the matter.

I nodded slowly. "I think that's what it was. Like he took what he wanted but knew ahead of time it was exactly what I needed."

Nikki grabbed my hand. "Girl, you are in trouble. Did you touch his shaved head? Bald guys are not my thing, but he's one I would make an exception for."

I dropped my head back, laughing. "Don't be ridiculous. It was a one-time thing. I'm working with those guys. They are my clients. It won't be happening again. I promise you."

She rolled her eyes. "Bullshit. Just wait. Now you've got a taste of each other. No turnin' back."

God, I loved Nikki, but she was so full of shit.

I held my hands up. "Okay, okay. Enough about me. What is your sexy story?"

She set her drink down like she always did when she wanted to concentrate, and proceeded to tell me a story that, if I'd heard it from her once, I'd heard it a hundred times.

"Remember that new doc I told you about? The one in pediatrics? Well, now his brother's working at the hospital, too, and they are probably a couple of the hottest hotties I've ever laid eyes on."

I seriously hoped I'd never have to go to a hospital for anything because from the stories Nikki told, all they did all day was fuck each other. It kind of creeped me out, come to think of it. How was that even slightly hygienic?

"Is that not the craziest thing you've ever heard?" she asked breathlessly.

Shit. I hadn't heard a word of what she'd said.

But I rolled with it. "Holy crap. That is something. You should write a book someday."

Her eyes widened. "You are so right. Damn. The stories I could tell."

She ordered us another round of drinks. "So. Did they remember you?"

Ah, yes. The inevitable shame. Hello, my friend! I might have kissed a hot rock star, but a few innocent words could somehow make me feel like shit all over again.

I looked down at my hands. "They did. It was pretty bad. The lead singer, Stone, just blurted out that I was, you know, the fat girl."

Nikki's mouth fell open. "What an ass."

But I squared my shoulders and lifted my chin. "I'm over it. Well, I will eventually get over it."

Yeah, right.

"You know, you can't let that shit follow you. Look at you now. You're gorgeous."

"Oh god, stop. Thank you, but stop," I said. "Don't things from your past haunt you?"

She got quiet for a change. "Yeah. For sure. I'm so afraid of being poor again, I'm fanatical about saving money. It's why I always seek out the cheap happy hour beers. And I barely buy any clothes because I can wear scrubs every day."

"Guess I'm not the only one, then," I said.

Her face brightened. "On a happier note, when can I meet the band? Can you get free concert tickets? Do you think they like nurses?"

## 16

## STONE

"Why are you still crashing at Ennis's house?"

Why did our manager give a shit where I lived? It was none of his business.

But I was trying not to be a dick, so I clenched my fists to control my usually out-of-control mouth.

"I don't know, Bryan. I know I have to get my own place since the ex booted me. But I just haven't felt like looking. Plus, who'd want to leave this place? Look at the goddamn view."

I gazed past the patio doors and the glittering swimming pool to the Hollywood sign in the distance.

When I was a kid, on the rare occasion my family drove from the boring-ass San Fernando Valley into the real LA, I couldn't wait to see the sign. It was an emblem of everything I didn't have and everything I wanted.

Back then, I kept thoughts like that to myself. We weren't encouraged to have dreams. In fact, my parents told my brother and me that it was fruitless for us to think we could do better. That we just weren't the 'type' to succeed at anything in particular.

*You're nothing special.*

Well. Fucking look at me now.

Parents' words, no matter how long ago they were spoken, never stray far from your mind. They just don't, no matter how much therapy you get and how much Jack Daniels you drink. I remember when I bought my first kick-ass house with my first royalty check from the record label, and how when I got the keys and the realtor left, I dropped to my knees in the foyer and just cried. A churning mishmash of both gratefulness and guilt will do that to you.

And when I had my first housewarming party, my parents weren't invited. Nor were they invited to any parties that followed.

That's right. They've never seen any place I'd lived. And I'm pretty sure they've never listened to any of my music.

They'd never give me that much credit for my hard work.

No wonder I was such a fuck up drunk.

Actually I couldn't blame everything on them, much

as I'd like to. My demons came in all shapes and sizes and from every damn direction.

Which was part of the reason I was sitting there with Dirty Bandit's manager on a day when I'd rather be out riding my motorcycle along the Pacific Coast Highway.

"This is an amazing place, I'll give you that, Stone," Bryan said. "But when you're ready to look, I'll get our realtor on board for you. She takes good care of us."

Whatever. She took awesome care of Bryan, that was for sure, from the looks of his sweet place. I used to think she was fucking him, but the truth is, I didn't think that was his jam.

Bryan, as much as he could be a pain in the ass, had always been there for us. Even though it chafed me to admit it, he was the driving force behind much of Dirty Bandit's success. Yeah, we worked goddamn hard—we had been since we were kids making music in whatever garage we could find to practice in—but when it came down to it, a lot of our success had to do with being in the right place at the right time.

Some might call that luck.

It was no joke.

I looked at other bands at the top of the charts. They were full of mega-talented musicians making amazing music.

So how come they weren't in our place?

It wasn't fair. But that's how it was.

And now the pressure—the unrelenting, merciless

pressure—to make every album better than the last, grew by the day.

That was why all I wanted to do was work on my music.

Wasn't that what it was all about?

Apparently not, I realized, as Coral James, our new publicist, joined Bryan and me in Ennis's living room.

I'd been suspicious the minute Ennis made an excuse to leave the house. Why did Bryan want only the two of us to meet with Coral? Was this some sort of intervention?

Because I didn't have time for that shit.

"Hi, Stone. Nice to see you again," she said, extending her hand once Bryan had let her in.

Holy shit. As much as I'd rather not have laid eyes on her ever again, she was a sight to behold.

Coral wasn't like all the other babes you saw around LA with their fake tits, spray on tans, and plumped-up lips. She was no less gorgeous, but her bright red hair and pale, pale skin were a stand-out.

She wasn't rail-thin like other LA girls, either. From what I could see, she had a big, juicy ass and nice little tits that bounced just the tiniest bit when she walked.

Today, her red hair was scraped up into a tight ponytail on top of her head. She wore a narrow skirt and a loose white shirt that looked like it might have belonged to some dude.

Did she have a husband? A boyfriend?

I'd forgotten to ask when I'd nailed her for being a

high school outcast. Not my proudest moment, and the second she left our meeting, both Ennis and Bryan had torn into me.

My big mouth had gotten me in trouble again.

But it was just so amazing, how much she'd changed.

Hugh, being the smooth, level-headed one, had swept her off to a late lunch.

Bastard.

But I could hand it to him. He wasn't much of a player, so when he stepped up his attentions to some pretty lady, I always said more power to him.

Wonder if he had a plan to get in her pants? Because I sure as hell would love to have a little fun with her.

"Hey, Coral. Thanks for coming back. Especially after my thoughtless remarks yesterday," I said.

I could own my shit. I wasn't that big of a dick.

She pulled her head back almost imperceptibly, clearly trying to downplay her surprise at my apology.

But I saw it. What I'd said had stung her, and she was in disbelief I was willing to admit my fuck up.

I could be an ass, but I also had enough brains to make things right when I did somebody wrong.

Most of the time, anyway.

## 17

## STONE

She smoothed out her skirt and took a seat on the sofa, settling into its corner so she could face Bryan and me. Rummaging through her bag, she pulled out a notebook and pen and began flipping through the pages.

Bryan leaned forward, elbows on knees. "What do you have for us, Coral?"

"And why did you want to meet with me alone, without the other guys?" I interrupted.

She stared me down. "Because I knew you'd be most resistant to our plans. So I wanted to run them by you, first."

I could work with that. I sat back in my chair satisfied. "All right then. Let's hear them."

"Okay. We had a brainstorm at the firm because I like to run my ideas past my colleagues. We came up with a three-prong strategy consisting of philanthropy, USO tours, and economic parity."

Jesus. If we did all that shit, we'd never have time to make music.

I took a deep breath, something I needed to do more often. "I get the philanthropy and USO tours, but what the hell is *economic parity*?"

She held a finger up. "I was just getting to that. Economic parity is when you work with your concert promoters to ensure that ticket prices are fair and affordable for all fans."

"How would it work?" Bryan asked.

"We'd negotiate that none of the ticket prices would go over a certain amount to make it fair, and that the service fees are kept to a minimum."

Shit. I didn't even know we could do that.

"This all sounds great, Coral, but I want to make sure the guys still have the time and energy to develop new music."

I stood up, too agitated to sit. "I don't know. This is a big fucking undertaking, and I'm not sure I'm down with it."

"Are you down with losing your contract with the label?" Coral asked, eyes blazing.

I didn't answer. I didn't have to answer.

I just wanted to focus on my goddamn music. But I knew arguing was a losing battle. Ennis and

Hugh would support whatever would keep the label happy.

I hated to call them sell-outs, but I'd never felt they were as dedicated to the music as I was.

Bryan nodded, clearly thrilled. "I have another thought, Coral, that the record label brought up to me in our last meeting. They're happy we brought you on board, and they're gonna love your new ideas. We can put a lot of this in motion pretty quickly. But we have an additional idea for the short term that I wanted to run by you."

She shrugged. "Let me have it. You know the firm's on board with whatever it takes to keep Dirty Bandit at the top of the charts."

What the hell was Bryan getting at? And if he had some brilliant idea, why hadn't he discussed this with the guys and me beforehand?

"We'd like you to travel with the band, Coral."

Dead silence. I could be mistaken, but I think the birds outside even stopped singing for a minute.

What the fucking fuck?

Irritated energy coursed through me, and against my best efforts, I loudly drummed my fingers on the chair when I sat back down.

I glanced over at Coral. Was she in on this?

But with one glance, I could see she wasn't and was just as surprised as me.

Actually, she was *more* surprised. And definitely horrified.

She looked like she might vomit. Kind of like how she looked when I brought up her high school years.

"Well. That's a radical idea, Bryan," she said slowly, pretending to ponder it.

I say *pretend* because it was clear there was no fucking way she wanted to travel with a rock band. And there was no fucking way we guys would want her to, either. No matter how good looking she was.

"Um, Bryan, I wasn't aware we needed a babysitter," I said, keeping my voice as level as possible. "Isn't that what we pay you for, to tour with us and make sure things go smoothly?"

But Bryan glared at me. "At the rate you're going, Stone, you're going to end up living in a trailer park without a penny or a friend to your name. So sit down and shut up."

Fuck me.

Coral held her hands up, attempting to defuse the situation. "Guys, calm down. I'll think about your suggestion, Bryan, and I'll take it back to Randall to get his take."

Bryan sat back in his seat, pleased that Coral hadn't come straight out and shot down his stupid fucking idea.

He glanced at his watch. "Oh darn, I gotta leave," he said, jumping to his feet. "I have to pick up Pixie from the groomer."

He dashed over to Coral and took her hand. "Thanks for everything, Coral. I'll talk to you later."

And he was gone.

Coral and I just sat looking at each other.

"Hey, you want a glass of wine?" I asked.

She looked at me and after a moment, shrugged one shoulder. "Sure. Why not?"

"Meet me out on the patio," I said, gesturing with my chin.

I joined her with a bottle of red and a couple glasses.

"So, Coral, are you gonna do it?" I asked, handing her a glass with a hefty pour.

She took a long draw on her wine. "Do what?" She settled back into her lounge chair and closed her eyes, letting the afternoon sun wash over her beautiful face.

"You know. Ride on the tour bus with us guys?"

Her eyes flew open in horror. "You guys take a bus? You don't fly?"

I stifled my laughter. "We *don't take a bus*, per se. We charter a big fancy one."

She dropped her head back wrinkled her nose. "Well. Still. No. I couldn't possibly go on tour with you."

Fucking A. I couldn't believe the Coral James sitting next to me was the same one from high school. It was just... incredible.

"We fly, too, of course. It's just that sometimes it's easier to take the bus when we're going to cities that aren't too far from each other."

"Well that makes sense. But I'm sure my boss won't

want me to be away from the office. We have too much going on. I just can't," she said, looking right at me for emphasis.

Damn. I was surprised by the disappointment that washed over me. Did I really want her along? Was I fucking crazy?

But what had I expected? Of course she wouldn't want to be stuck in what was essentially a rolling hotel room with three guys she probably hated.

I leaned closer to her. "Coral. I think it's a good thing you're on board with us."

"No way," she said, laughing. "Are you kidding?"

"I… I'm not always the easiest person to work with. Or even to be around. It's the stress. The constant pressure to keep producing better and better music. Sometimes, I feel like it's strangling me."

Listening, she set her wine glass down.

She nodded slowly. "I can see that. I can't imagine what it would be like."

Fuck. Why had I told her that? I didn't need to be baring my soul to anyone, much less someone I hardly knew.

What was I saying? I didn't know her *at all.*

I cleared my throat and stood, my gaze hovering over the terra cotta rooftops below and downtown LA in the distance.

"C'mon. Let's go for a swim."

I dropped my jeans to the ground and dove in.

## 18

## CORAL

Holy shit. Stone McIntyre didn't wear underwear.

He was a free-baller, as they say. And how did I know this? He'd just dropped trou and dove into the pool we were sitting next to.

He was naked.

As in not a stitch of clothing. And I'd seen the package. My client's package.

I'd not started the day, or even the week, thinking I might ever see one of my clients naked. It was just not something that happened in my field.

If you were a doctor, you might see your patients naked.

If you were a masseuse, you might see your clients naked.

If you managed a gym, you might see your members naked.

Not so much in PR.

And now I was supposed to join him? In the water? Without a bathing suit?

Stone broke the surface with a holler after swimming the entire length of the pool underwater.

"Damn, this feels great. C'mon in, Coral!" He dove back under and did a handstand.

Oh my god. I looked down into my wine glass, wishing I could unsee, um... *that*. Stone had flipped to his back, gently swooshing his hands to stay afloat. And he was moving toward the edge of the pool closest to me.

With his, you know, *dick* bobbing in the water.

*Coral, meet Stone's penis...*

I supposed when working with rock stars, this sort of thing was par for the course. I should have been prepared. I knew they were kind of hedonistic, so it had been just a matter of time until I was faced with some sort of indiscretion.

I just hadn't expected it so soon.

And I was supposed to ride in a tour bus with these guys?

Cripes, if they weren't used to having a woman on board, god knew how they behaved in an enclosed space.

"Hey. Are you coming in?" Stone asked.

I dared a peek in his direction and was relieved to see he was no longer on his back on the surface of the water. He was holding on to the edge of the pool, his muscular shoulders and tattooed arms glistening wet, his light hair darkened by the water and slicked back from his forehead to show off his perfect bone structure.

Holy shit.

"Oh, I think I'll pass," I said cheerfully.

I hoped he hadn't noticed I'd spilled red wine down my white blouse.

"Come on. I won't look while you jump in. The pool's heated. It's amazing." True to his word, he turned from me and swam to the other side of the pool where he focused on the view.

Well, shit. I looked around. No one else was home. But did I really want to skinny dip with Stone McIntyre?

No, I did not. But I could paddle around in my underwear. For just a few minutes. Then I'd head home.

"All right. Keep looking away." I kicked off my shoes, let my skirt fall to the ground, and tossed my blouse on the lounge chair.

Damn. He wasn't lying. The water *was* incredible.

"Wow," I yelled when I surfaced.

"What are you wearing?" he asked, turning around.

"My bra and panties. You have a problem with that?"

He laughed and splashed me. "Nah. That's smart. I probably would have kept my boxers on... if I'd remembered to wear any." He laughed and did a somersault.

His playfulness put me at ease. It was incredible to see this side of him when the tabloids only showed him fighting and being carted off in handcuffs. Well, and screaming into the mic at stadium concerts with tens of thousands of fans watching.

I swam to the center of the pool and treaded water. As entertaining as he was, I wanted to keep a safe distance. It wouldn't do for him to get the wrong idea.

Although Hugh had gotten the wrong idea the day before, and it sure as hell had turned out fun.

"The sun's going down. Check it out," Stone said, resting his arms on the edge of the pool.

I paddled up next to him and propped my own elbows on the pool's edge.

"Wow. So beautiful."

Holy crap. Just yesterday I'd been transported back to my life as an awkward teenager by Stone's thoughtless words, and now here I was, swimming with him and watching the sunset.

And thinking maybe he *wasn't* the biggest asshole in the universe.

But the jury was still out.

He looked my way. "It is beautiful. Like you," he said, reaching to move a strand of hair from my forehead.

Oh god.

And just like that, his lips were on mine, soft and gentle at first, and then hard and demanding, just like the way he lived his life. With one elbow propped on the edge of the pool, he wove his fingers through my wet hair enough to pull me to him.

And he suddenly stopped, leaning his forehead against mine in an unexpectedly intimate gesture.

No.

I had to go. Like get the hell out of the pool and get the hell out of this house. I'd kissed Hugh the day before, and now Stone. What would they think of me?

I'm sure they had women throwing themselves at them all the time. Surely, they could easily find someone willing and able to serve their needs.

Because I sure as hell wasn't going to.

"I'll see you later," I said, swimming past him to the pool's ladder.

But just as I did, I brushed against his erect penis.

Oh please god, don't let him float on his back right now.

I scrambled up the ladder and turned to find Stone's gaze running over me. I scooped up a thick, white towel, wrapped it around myself and gathered my things.

Just before I left, I turned to see him treading water in the middle of the pool.

"See ya later, Coral. Thanks for the meeting and... stuff." Then he turned back toward the sunset and we each caught the last couple seconds of it.

## 19

## CORAL

"Jesus, Coral. How bad could it be?"

This was not happening. My boss, one of the people I looked up to most, was putting the screws to me.

Did I look like a fucking groupie? Did I look like someone who stayed up all hours of the night drinking and smoking god-knows-what, only to do it all over again the next day?

I knew how rockers lived, even if I didn't listen to their music. And while I'd finally accepted the inevitability having these guys as clients, I sure as hell didn't want to share accommodations with them.

In fact, I didn't want to stay anywhere *near* them, and I certainly did not want to go on tour with them.

But Randall didn't see it like I did. And next thing I knew, he was driving me to Los Angeles International Airport to fly to Chicago. I'd meet the guys there, where I'd join them in their tour bus.

I didn't know which was worse—the bus or the guys. But together, they left me horrified.

And feeling like I was going to vomit.

He pulled up to the departures curb and smiled. "Coral. I know you're not crazy about this arrangement. But please give it a try. Bryan feels like the guys respect you enough to listen to you and stay out of trouble. If it's horrible after a few days, let me know and you can come home."

Gee, thanks. I didn't know *sacrificial lamb* was part of my job description.

"Here's your ticket. A driver will pick you up in Chicago so you can rendezvous with the rest of the band."

The horror on my face must have been pretty obvious.

"Coral. It will be fine. Now get going. You'll miss your flight."

I grabbed my wheelie suitcase from the back seat and slammed Randall's door as hard as I could for emphasis.

He was going to owe me for this. Big time.

By the time I exited arrivals at Chicago O'Hare and found the driver with the sign bearing my name, I'd worked myself into such a tizzy I could barely speak.

The flight had given me the perfect amount of time to torment myself, thinking about how terrible the next few days of my life were going be—sharing a bus with three guys who thought their shit didn't stink.

*What would I do for privacy?*

*Where would I go to the bathroom?*

*How would I do my job?*

*Where would I sleep?*

The list went on and on, and each time it got longer, I was that much closer to losing my mind.

"How far is the meeting point?" I asked the driver.

He pointed. "Just up here, ma'am."

Shit. Maybe I could fake sick. Or trip and break my leg. Either of those would give me the perfect reason to turn around and head back home, right?

"Miss James, here we go," the driver said, jerking me out of my tortured reverie. "I see Bryan right over there. Let me take you and your things to him."

Did he have his dog with him? Really?

"Coral is here!" Bryan yelled like I was his long-lost buddy.

He actually threw his arms around me while Pixie humped my leg.

I patted his back until he let me go.

Jesus. What was I in for?

"Why are there two buses?" I asked.

He gestured toward the first. "This one is for Stone, Ennis, and Hugh. That one over there is for the rest of the band, all the equipment, and me. And of course little Pixie." He picked her up and kissed her drooly mouth.

The buses did look big and luxurious.

I headed toward the equipment bus. I wanted to get my bag underneath before they closed everything up.

But Bryan caught my arm. "Oh, Coral, over here. You're riding in the bus with the guys."

20

---

CORAL

Was this just *shit on Coral month*? Seriously, universe. What did I do wrong? Who did I offend so badly?

I held on to the handle of my wheelie bag for balance. Falling over in front of a client was never a good move.

"Um, Bryan, no way am I going to be the only one to ride with the guys." I continued walking toward the equipment bus.

This shit was non-negotiable.

That's when I felt his hand on my arm. "Coral, there's no room for you on the equipment bus. You have to ride with the guys in the front."

He must have noticed I was green around the gills.

"I'm sorry. But there's no other way. Adding you at the last minute like this didn't give us many options."

Well, fuck me.

I took a deep breath. It wouldn't do to go postal on a client. "Okay. I understand. But why don't *you* ride with them?"

He put his hands on his hips—perhaps signaling that he'd already thought this through? "The point of having you on the tour, Coral, is that you wield a different sort of authority over the guys than me or anyone else. We feel you can keep them in line."

Stone was right. I *was* a babysitter.

I didn't get paid enough for this shit and would be bringing this up to Randall next time I saw him.

I wheeled my ass over to the guys' bus where the driver smiled at me and grabbed my bag from me. I hoisted my tote on my shoulder, and forced myself to climb the bus's narrow steps, as if on a death march. One foot in front of the other, and repeat.

When I got to the top step and turned the corner, I found Hugh, Stone, and Ennis sitting on an uphol-stered banquette.

Doing shots. With rock music blaring in the background.

Thank god I'd brought ear plugs *and* a good set of headphones.

A quick scan proved the bus to be nice enough, not that I was any more pleased about being there. The dark paneling, cushy seating, and multiple TV screens made it seem somewhat civilized.

Luxury on a bus. Yeah, right.

"Coral's here!" Stone yelled. "Get over here and have a shot with us."

Here we go.

Dropping my tote, I approached the table and Ennis scooted over to make room for me. I gladly grabbed a seat next to him. After all, he was the only one who hadn't tried to kiss me. I needed to keep shit professional.

"Bottoms up!" Stone shouted as the three guys downed shots of Jack Daniels.

As soon as he was done, he jumped up and pulled a clean glass from the cupboard. He filled it, and pushed it toward me.

All eyes were on me.

Oh god. I didn't do shots of anything.

"Oh, I don't know guys. I have some work to do," I said, pushing it back in Stone's direction.

They shrugged, looking at each other. And poured themselves another.

Oh what the fuck.

I grabbed the shot I'd just pushed away and, holding my breath, forced the whiskey down my throat. I coughed and sputtered from the harsh burn.

Ugh. Gross. How could people do this for fun?

I was only doing it under duress.

"Oh shit, Coral. You okay?" Ennis asked.

"Yeah. I'm good," I gagged, dabbing at my watering eyes.

All eyes were on me. Of course the dork from their high school years couldn't handle a little shot of whiskey.

I was tempted to take another just to show them. Show them what, I wasn't sure. Maybe that my dork years were behind me?

So I did.

Bryan poked his head into the bus, holding Pixie to his chest. "We're leaving in a few. You guys show Coral around yet?"

Stone laughed. "Hey Coral. That's the front of the bus," he said, pointing. "And over there is the back."

Bryan rolled his eyes and climbed the rest of the steps. "Coral, that door over there is the bathroom and shower. All the way in the back, behind that curtain, are the bunks. Yours has your name on it."

"Yeah, you got the good bunk, Coral," Ennis said.

Was this a joke?

There was a *good* bunk?

"How could any bunk be a good bunk?" I asked.

The four men looked at each other for a moment, and then all burst out laughing.

Bryan shook his head. "You have a great sense of humor, Coral. Okay everybody, we'll be hitting the road in just a moment."

I hadn't meant that to be a joke.

"Oh, and Coral, there are sandwiches and other munchies in the fridge over there," he added, pointing.

Sandwiches. Yay.

"It won't be too bad, Cor," Stone assured me, downing another shot.

Great. Stuck on a bus with a bunch of drunk guys who think they can give me a nickname.

"So you guys pretty much just sit here and drink from one city to the next?" I asked with a smirk.

My, the Jack was making me salty.

Stone guffawed. "Yup. That's all we do, along with watching porn and jerking each other off."

OhMyGod.

"He's joking, Coral," Hugh said. "Just ignore him. He likes to haze people."

"Speaking of jerking off, Coral, were you getting laid in high school?"

## 21

## CORAL

Oh no he didn't.

"Speaking of jerking off, Stone, why don't you go fuck yourself—" I started to say.

Oh crap. Not the way to talk to a client.

"Yeah, Stone, shut the hell up," Ennis said, pouring another round of shots.

No more for me. Absolutely not.

"Hey, Coral, I have a meeting with a personal trainer in the morning. Want to work out with us?" Ennis asked. "Stone and Hugh are too pussy to join."

His friends rolled their eyes.

If I were going to work out, I'd better put a stop to the shot drinking.

"Sure. Okay."

"Yeah, you former fatties better start doing some jumping jacks," Stone laughed.

Asshole.

Ennis and I looked at each other. I did remember him being a little… soft. Hardly what I would call over-weight. Or as the asshole put it—a fatty.

"Hey, Coral, did you hear Stone wrote a book? It's called *I'm a Douche and I Know It*," Ennis said.

Everyone erupted into peals of laughter. Everyone that was, except for Stone.

I had no idea how I would survive this.

"Well," Stone said, stretching. "I'm gonna watch *The Big Lebowski*. Anyone want to join me?"

Hugh rolled his eyes. "Again? How many times have you seen that?"

Stone left the banquette and settled into one of the cushy recliners. Grabbing a headset and pulling it over his ears, he said, "Not enough, Hugh. Not enough."

Ennis rose from his seat. "I'm going to read my book," he said, and disappeared to what I guessed was his own bunk.

Somehow, the music in the bus got magically quieter. I needed to know where the control for that was. It was a matter of survival.

"Well, I know this probably isn't your idea of fun, Coral, but we're glad you're on the team," Hugh said, once we were alone.

Guess he didn't want to say that in front of the other guys?

"Thanks. Looking forward to seeing one of your shows." I nearly gagged at my lie.

"Have you ever been backstage at a concert? It's pretty cool," he said.

I shook my head, thinking back to what my high school self would have thought about riding a tour bus with these guys, and hanging out at one of their concerts.

But more importantly, what did my grown-up self think about all this? The guys might have still thought I was a dork—I didn't give a shit.

Maybe being on the bus with them was a good thing. A chance to show them the new me. And what they'd missed out on all those years ago.

After an egg salad sandwich, I made my way back to my bunk, holding the walls to remain upright in the lurching vehicle, hoping the internet access they'd promised actually worked. I had things to do, even if I had consumed a couple shots of Jack Daniels and was exhausted.

It turned out that the bunks were pretty spacious. Someone had put my small wheelie bag at the foot of my bed, leaving plenty of room to stretch out, change, and do some work. I stepped into the bunk and drew the privacy curtain closed. I pulled on some PJ bottoms and a T-shirt and opened my laptop. But in minutes, I was dozing off to the gentle rocking motion of the bus and its quiet roar underneath us.

I don't know how much later I was woken by a moaning sound.

What the hell was that? Was someone sick? Too much whisky?

I grabbed my phone to check the time. Three a.m. Crap. The battery in my laptop, still sitting open, had died. And I'd gotten no work done.

What was going on out there? I inched my privacy curtain back, but all the lights in the bus were out. The section where the driver sat was curtained off to block any light from the road.

I tucked back into my bunk and closed my eyes, but it started up again. What the hell was that?

"Ohhhh..."

Okay. That wasn't a sick person.

Holy shit. Was one of the guys jerking off?

Ew.

Jerking off was fine, but if you were not alone, wouldn't you keep it quiet?

I poked my head out of the bunk again and realized the noise was coming from just above me. Because I'd gone to sleep first, I had no idea which guy was up there. Could it be Ennis? Or maybe Hugh?

But I had to say, picturing any of the guys, even bigmouth Stone, stroking himself was kind of... hot.

I turned over and tried to ignore the noise. I really

did. But the throbbing between my legs was not letting me.

So I slipped my fingers into my PJ bottoms. I ran my fingers between my lips, zeroing in on my clit for some sweet release.

Lulled by the motion of the bus and my kisses from Hugh and Stone just a couple days before, I went to town on my aching sex. When a final grunt reached me from the top bunk, my own orgasm exploded. I writhed through the waves that poured over me, as if I were back in that swimming pool with Stone.

I should be able to sleep, now.

I rolled over on my side, and just as I started to doze, someone stuck their head under my bunk curtain.

"Hey, Coral. You awake?"

## 22

# ENNIS

I blinked in the dark, trying to see Coral's face.

"I heard you tossing and turning. I can't sleep either. Wanna talk? We can go up to the front of the bus," I whispered.

She sat up, yawning and rubbing her eyes.

Hadn't she already been awake? Whatever.

"Oh. Hi, Ennis. Okay," she said, swinging her legs over the edge of the bunk.

We settled into seats around the table where we'd been drinking earlier, and I lit a small candle.

"That's nice," she said, gazing around the dim bus interior. "It almost looks like a hotel room in the dark."

God did she look cute in her pajama pants and

skimpy top. Her hair was mussed, and when she caught me looking at it, she gathered it in front of one shoulder, and started making a loose braid.

I tore my gaze away. No need to make her uncomfortable. It was pretty obvious she'd rather be anywhere other than a tour bus with us three guys, and I didn't want to make it worse for her.

Especially considering the Perry High School past we shared.

"Does it suck, to be here with us?" I asked.

Even in the lousy light, I could see her stiffen. I braced myself for her canned, professional answer. After all, the woman probably wanted to keep her job.

Instead, she shrugged. "I'm not entirely comfortable with it. But I like my bunk. It's cozy, like a little space pod or something. Do you like these tour buses?"

I looked at the candlelight crawling over the ceiling and bus walls. "I do. Something about them makes me feel like a real rocker, you know? They're cramped and all, but they also feel... authentic or something."

That probably sounded lame as hell, but if I pointed out the positives, maybe she'd be more at ease.

"I even sleep a little better on the buses, I think from the motion. Well, usually, anyway. See, I have terrible insomnia. That's part of the reason why they hired me a trainer. Everything else has failed—shrinks, antidepressants, massage, meditation—now they want me to work out."

Whoa. I didn't normally share this side of myself

and wasn't sure why the hell I was now. I barely knew Coral. But something about it being late at night in the confines of the bus, in the middle of god knew where, with the future of the band in jeopardy, made me feel lonely.

"I'd think the drinking is probably not helping," she said.

Bingo.

While I was surprised to hear her say those blunt words, I knew as well as anyone she was right.

"Yeah. I've cut back. But not enough, I guess. I gotta make more changes." I stared at the candle flame. "I can't lose Dirty Bandit, Coral. It's everything to me. Basically, it's my life."

To my surprise, she reached for my hand, her fingers gripping mine.

We were silent for a moment, relaxed by the rocking of the bus.

"I lost my little sister," I blurted out.

Jesus, what was wrong with me?

She leaned toward me. "What about your sister?"

In the dim light, I closed my eyes. "I was driving my little sister home after a show a few years ago. We had the radio cranked and were singing at the top of our lungs. I wasn't really paying attention and—"

I couldn't continue.

So she did.

"There was an accident, Ennis?"

Eyes still closed, I nodded. Arianna had been my

buddy. I could still remember her as a little kid, begging to come to our band practice, where she would dance around, pretending to be singing into a microphone. When she got older, she'd bring her friends and they'd watch us for hours, nudging each other and giggling. She'd been my biggest supporter.

Even after several years, the pain was still a stake through my heart.

"Is that her name tattooed there?" she asked, pointing to the inside of my forearm.

"Yeah. Arianna."

"I'd thought that was a girlfriend or something. Good lord. I'm so sorry."

And... I'd pretty much just ruined the mood.

Coral picked up on the awkwardness of our silence and started talking about all the things she was setting up for the band.

"How are we going to do all that? It just doesn't sound possible," I said. Charity concerts, USO travel, talk show appearances. Jesus. I was already tired all the time.

She laughed. "Well, we're not gonna do them all at once. They'll be spaced out over several months. I'll arrange it all. You pretty much just show up and look good."

I stretched and yawned.

"Getting sleepy?" she asked, still holding my hand.

"God, I hope so. We meet with the trainer in just a few hours."

"Well. Glad to know I can put you to sleep," she said with a small laugh.

"What? You should feel good about helping me relax."

Yawning, Coral stood to return to her bunk. But I didn't release her hand. I couldn't.

As she sat back down, I lifted it to my lips, brushing over her skin and inhaling her soft scent. God, I could have stayed like that all night.

While Coral watched, full of surprise, I reached for her other hand and pulled her to me. If she pushed me away, so be it.

I'd back off.

But I hoped I wouldn't have to.

Her eyes fluttered closed, and she tilted her head to give me access to her neck. I shouldn't have been making the moves on her, but I wasn't exactly at the top of my game in the early morning hours, starved for sleep, heading toward god knew what city.

So instead of calling it a night, I found her lips, urgently exploring, hungry for connection.

"You're so beautiful, Coral. I haven't been able to stop thinking about you since our first meeting."

It was true. I hadn't. That goddamn green dress...

"Ennis? Ennis, I need to tell you something," she said in a whisper.

ENNIS

Oh Christ. Here it comes.

She had a boyfriend. Maybe even a fiancé.

I placed my hands on either side of her lovely face. "What is it?"

Her words tumbled out like a terrible confession. "I... I've kissed Hugh and Stone in the last few days. I thought you should know. I don't want you guys to get the wrong idea."

I chuckled and lay her back on the bench where we were sitting.

"It's fine, Coral. It's fine."

I knew her thinking. She was worried we'd consider her a slut, that we'd see her as another band groupie wanting to fuck a celebrity so she could brag about it to her friends.

But that wasn't the case with Coral. Not by a long shot. And she was going to learn that.

I slipped my fingers into the waistband of her PJ bottoms and slowly began to drag them toward her knees, inch by inch. I knew not to make any fast movements so she'd have the chance to send me away if she wanted.

But she lay back, her breath deepening as she relaxed.

Dying to get to her bare pussy, I parted her knees just enough, and when I pressed my tongue between her folds, she was as soft and delicious as I knew she'd be, her scent revealing her excitement. Roaming through her swollen lips, I was on the verge of another world. One I never wanted to leave.

"Oh god, Ennis. That's so good," she murmured as I slowly lapped her from clit to ass and back.

I entered her with one finger and made a *come here* motion against her walls. She gasped and arched into me.

So fucking hot.

"Come for me, baby. I want to feel you come."

I sped up the motion of my finger as well as the swirl of my tongue, and with a gasp, she began to tremble. I had to hold her with my free hand to keep her from tumbling off the banquette onto the floor. Her head thrashed from side to side, her back arching further, pushing her sex more deeply into my mouth.

I was in heaven.

And I was pretty sure she was enjoying herself, too.

She clamped a hand over her mouth to stifle her moans. I wasn't sure it did any good. And I didn't care.

As she caught her breath, I looked up and found she'd lifted her tank top to play with her tits. They were perky and pink-tipped, and the way she pulled her nipples nearly made me come right there in my boxer shorts.

And I'd just jerked off thirty minutes earlier.

"Fucking awesome, baby," I said.

I would have loved to experience more of her, but I could tell from the swinging window shade that the sun was coming up outside.

So I leaned to kiss her so she could taste what I had enjoyed so much.

And she suddenly shoved me away.

What the?

"Holy fuck," she yelled.

I followed her gaze over my shoulder to where Hugh stood, looking right down at her.

Uh-oh. I could have told him that might not go over well.

"What are you doing?" she hissed, pulling her top down and her pants up. "What the fuck? Were you just standing there watching us?"

I could barely see him but was able to make out a

slight smile. He nodded politely. "Yes, I was watching, but—"

She turned to me. "Was this a set up? Did you tell him you were going to try and get in my pants and that he should keep an eye out to enjoy the show?"

She frantically looked from one of us to the other, fury distorting her pretty face.

"You guys are fuckers," she spat.

"Coral. Just a minute, okay?" I said, stretching for her hand.

But she jumped out of my reach too fast.

"I do not appreciate this," she sputtered, backing up. "I should have known better than to trust you. Any of you."

Hugh held up his hands. "Coral. We like you. And yes, we have discussed you, although this, just now, wasn't a set up. I was going to take a piss and heard you guys. You looked so fucking hot, lying there, with Ennis licking your—"

"STOP," she shrieked, shaking her head and backing away.

"Look, Coral. I didn't mean to upset you. I'm sorry. It's just that we guys... we like to share."

I wanted to tell Hugh it wasn't the best time to spring our 'interesting' proclivities on Coral, but too late.

He'd played our hand a little too soon.

"*Share*? What the hell does that mean? Never mind, I don't care. I'm glad you both had a fun evening at my expense. Now you can go back to your bunks and jerk off all you want. I'm going to bed, and don't you dare come around, or I'll deck you so hard you won't be able to sing for a week."

Damn. She had it in her. And I liked that. In fact, my hard-on, which had begun to subside, had sprung back to attention at her outburst.

"Coral, we'd never—" I started.

But she whipped around and stuck a finger in my face. "YOU. Shut. The. Fuck. Up."

Christ.

She stormed off to the back of the bus and jumped into her bunk, yanking the curtains shut and snapping them closed.

"Jesus," Hugh said. "She thinks we planned this? If we were only so smart." He chuckled quietly.

"Shhh," I told him. It wouldn't do for her to think we were mocking her on top of everything else.

I felt like shit. The last thing I'd intended was to throw her for such a loop.

"Hopefully by morning she will have cooled off. I mean, dude, you shouldn't have helped yourself to our little session. It was way too soon."

Shit. It already *was* morning.

"Sorry, man. I didn't think she'd flip like that. I didn't even think she'd notice, she was coming so hard. That was hot as fuck."

I headed to my own bunk.

It *had* been hot. Actually, beyond hot, being with

such a beautiful, spunky woman in such an intimate way. But she wasn't some groupie who'd fought her way onto the bus for some late-night fun. We were supposed to be working with Coral, improving our reputation.

That's when I realized the late-night fun was going to be a one-time-only thing.

## 24

## CORAL

A bunch of fucking idiots was what those guys were, and I fell right into their trap. Probably just like every other female who crossed their paths and spread her legs at the snap of their fingers.

I was a fucking idiot. That's all there was to it. What had I been thinking to let Ennis slide my PJ bottoms down so he could go to town on me? What kind of smart girl does that?

Was I trying to prove something? Prove that I was cool—no longer the one who sat in the corner of the school cafeteria with the other outcasts?

*I wanna prove myself so badly, I'll let you eat me…*

What if Randall found out? I mean, not the gory details but just that I'd been... canoodling... with the guys. He'd lose all respect for me, and most likely fire my pathetic ass.

I could see it now.

*Sorry, Coral, but we can't have you fucking around with the clients. Lunch is one thing but pulling down your pants is another...*

I punched my pillow.

Why, why, why?

And how did I end up putting on a goddamn show for Hugh? What the hell was that all about?

Every fiber of my being had been screaming *get your ass back to bed.* That nothing good was going to come of messing around with Ennis, or any of the guys for that matter, late at night on a bus tearing across America's highways.

But the stress of recent days and the strangeness of my situation rendered me unable—actually, unwilling —to resist.

Plain and simple, I wanted it. I wanted Ennis, the beautiful, vulnerable, driven, guilt-ridden man, to make me feel good. I wanted to forget where we were —even *who* we were—for just a little while.

*It's fine* he'd whispered, as he'd laid me back on the bench.

And it had been fine, at least initially. *So* fine. Like nothing I'd ever experienced *fine.* The few other guys who'd gone down on me in my past had been abject failures compared to Ennis, with their slobbery spit and general sexual incompetence.

All thoughts of consequences had evacuated my brain. And consideration of the past or future—well, they didn't exist at that moment in time.

I didn't say no because I didn't fucking want to.

That's how you end up messing around with a hot client. I'm sure it happened all the time.

But it didn't happen to me all the time. Or ever, for that matter. It's why I was Going Places, according to Randall. I knew how to behave. Get the job done. Make clients happy.

I guess I did just make a couple clients happy, now that I thought about it.

The very clients I was supposed to be babysitting, keeping them on the straight and narrow, and ensuring they didn't lose their record contract.

After all, didn't my employment depend on their employment?

If Dirty Bandit were out of business, well, Coral James would be out of business, too.

If I fucked this up, our firm's name would be mud. And I'd be out of a job. It didn't matter how much Randall liked or respected me. Someone would have to take the fall for the failure, and better me than him.

As I struggled to fall asleep—which was stupid because I knew the more I struggled, the less likely it was that I would—I tried to think of what I could do for a living if I got booted from the firm.

No one else in public relations would hire me. That was certain. I'd have to come up with something completely different.

I could talk to Nikki. See how she liked nursing, aside from messing around with hot doctors.

Actually, scratch that. I hated blood. And touching strangers. And nasty smells.

I could never be a nurse.

Dog walker. I could be a dog walker. Wasn't that the fallback for people who didn't know what else to do?

But I didn't really like dogs, either.

I drifted off, imagining picking up the poop of annoying little animals like Bryan's Pixie.

"Coral!" someone was calling.

I opened my eyes to the morning sun. Holy shit. I'd fallen asleep after all, if only for a few hours.

I unsnapped my bunk curtain and stuck my head out. All three guys were in the front of the bus, sitting around the banquette where Ennis and I had put on a little show for Hugh the night before.

"What?" I asked.

Ennis stuck his head around the corner like nothing had ever happened. "Trainer's here. You have five to get ready."

I plopped back on my pillow. I'd barely slept. I didn't know how I could face Ennis and Hugh. And the worst part was, there was nowhere to hide.

Maybe I could spend the rest of my time hunkered down in my little pod, and as soon as we hit a big city, have the bus driver drop me at an airport?

But there was the job thing. And the fact that I wanted to keep it, if at all possible.

"Be right there," I called, and rummaged through my suitcase for sneakers and leggings.

"Here's a cap," Ennis said, pushing a Dirty Bandit hat down on my head as we left the bus. "It's getting warm out and you'll be sweating."

His own hair was pulled back into a ponytail, and he wore only board shorts and running shoes.

Whatever.

I exited the bus without acknowledging any of them.

Once in the bright sunshine, I pulled my new cap lower. Ennis was good for something.

A beefy guy in expensive running shoes approached me. "Hey! You must be Coral! I'm Jock."

"Our trainer," Ennis added.

"Hey, Jack," I grumbled.

"Not Jack. *Jock.*"

No way. A trainer whose name was actually *Jock*?

"Nice to meet you," I said.

"Okay, guys," Jock said, looking me up and down, "let's take a slow jog around this track here for a little warm up."

I let the guys lead the way because, one, I wanted to

see how fast Ennis could go, and second, I didn't want them staring at my ass.

After not even one lap, Jock dropped back to run next to me. "Hey, Coral."

Ugh. Couldn't I just work out in peace?

I looked at him and forced a small smile, then returned to stare at the track in front of me.

But he was not deterred. "I'm glad you could join us today."

"Thank you."

"How long have you been traveling with the band? Are you somebody's girlfriend?"

"Huh?" My head spun so fast in his direction that I stumbled off the track and started to go down.

But Jock saved me. Because, of course.

"Whoa there, little lady." He held my arm until I had my balance back. "You okay?"

No, I was not okay. But I sure as hell wasn't going to tell him that.

"I'm fine. And I'm not anybody's girlfriend. I'm the band's publicist. I just got on the bus yesterday."

There, jerk. You had the whole story.

"Oooooh, I see," he said, smacking his head as he realized he should have kept his damn mouth shut.

He must have noticed the intense stink eye I'd thrown in his direction, because he kept digging himself in deeper trying to recover. "Usually the girls they have on the bus are groupies and such."

Great. Fucking great.

I picked up my speed, not because I thought I could outrun him, which I obviously could not, but because I wanted to burn off some of my shit mood. And get rid of Jock.

But he didn't take the hint. He picked up speed too, and kept on talking.

"So, you live in LA, like the guys do. Have you ever been to Universal Studios? I've always wanted to go there."

"Nope," I said. "Never been."

"Really?" he exclaimed in disbelief. "How about Disney?"

"Yeah. Went once when I was a kid. You know, Jock. I think I'm gonna head back to the bus. Thanks for the jog," I said, turning and picking up speed. I didn't want him trying to change my mind.

"Oh, okay, Coral. Nice meeting you!" he called after me.

I ran up the steps to the bus, only to find Bryan sitting at the banquette, where he was letting little Pixie drink from his coffee cup.

"Coral, good morning. How was the workout?" he asked cheerfully. "Coffee?"

I held my hand up to say *no*. "I called it quits early. Um, got a side stitch."

Hugh was stretched out on the bench seats lining the side of the bus, reading the newspaper. He looked up from his reading and nodded like nothing had happened the night before. Stone was opposite him, wearing headphones and watching something on his iPad. He raised a hand to wave.

I'd bet anything he told Stone he'd watched Ennis and me. That's just the kind of people these guys were.

So I acted like nothing had ever happened, either.

## 25

## CORAL

Bryan put his hands on his hips, surveying the calm. "Just as well. The new drivers just arrived. As soon as Ennis is back, we're hitting the road." He disappeared down the bus steps.

I grabbed my toiletries from my bunk and headed for the small shower I'd seen in the restroom.

"Hey guys, do you know where I can find a towel?"

"In that cupboard over there," Hugh said, pointing. "Take as many as you want. Someone comes in and cleans and replaces them with new ones."

I grabbed a couple fluffy white towels and locked the bathroom door behind me. I twisted my hair up and took a quick shower, then put on jeans, a T-shirt, and some high-heeled boots. What else would one wear traveling with a rock band?

Just as I exited the bathroom, Ennis returned, pink-faced and drenched in sweat.

And looking hotter than ever. Damn him. He nodded at me.

Like nothing ever happened. Did these guys do this stuff so often it was business as usual?

"En, we're hitting the road in a few," Hugh said.

Ennis reached into a mini-fridge and pulled out a bottle of water. "Why'd you bail, Coral?"

"Got a cramp."

He sucked down his water and tossed the bottle in the trash. He kicked off his shoes, peeled off his soaked shirt, and dropped his shorts to the floor.

And no, he wasn't wearing any underwear.

"Shit. Forgot a towel," he said, brushing past me.

I looked away.

Well. These guys sure didn't worry about a little thing like modesty.

As soon as Ennis entered the bathroom, Bryan popped his head back into the bus.

Jesus, this place was busy.

"I see Ennis is back. Let's hit the road." He turned to leave but stopped short.

"Coral, can you step outside with me for a moment?"

Did *he* know what had happened, too?

I shielded my eyes from the bright sun.

"Hey, I forgot to tell you. As you know, we'll be in New York City later tonight after the show in Philly. We're booked into the Four Seasons."

Ohthankgod.

I felt like I'd just won the lottery.

"Great, Bryan."

"I'm still gonna ask you to keep an eye on the guys, though, okay?" he asked.

My spirits, briefly lifted at the words *Four Seasons*, began to fall back to the shitty place they'd been for nearly twenty-four hours.

"Oh. Right. Of course."

He didn't miss my disappointment. "You'll have your own room, but it will be adjoined with the guys' suite. We need to try to keep their partying under control. And if they bring back women, just keep them quiet and get the girls out of there early."

What the fucking fuck?

I was doing nothing of the sort.

Especially since *I* was one of those women he was talking about. I wasn't a groupie, of course, but I'd fallen prey to the charms of Ennis so easily I may as well have been.

"Sure. Will do," I said, defeated. I turned to head back into the bus.

"Oh, Coral?"

"Yes, Bryan?" I said, stopping.

"Thank you."

Yeah, yeah.

"One more thing," he called. "Would you like Pixie to ride with you guys?" He kissed the top of her head.

Was he freaking kidding?

"No, that's ok. I'm so clumsy and in such a small space I'm afraid I might step on her," I lied.

Once the bus started rolling and the guys were either reading or, in Stone's case, watching a movie, I went over our New York schedule. I called the producer of Good Day New York, where the guys would appear on the city's popular morning show.

He answered on the first ring. "Daniel Waters here."

"Daniel, it's Coral James with Dirty Bandit. Just wanting to make sure all is a go for the band's guest appearance," I said.

Hugh looked up at me with a raised eyebrow and returned to his reading.

They could blame me all they wanted for setting them up with a cheesy morning show, but they had only themselves to blame for their shit reputations, which I was now charged with shining up.

Daniel rustled some papers in the background, and clicked on a computer keyboard. "Dirty Bandit. Yes. Everything looks great. Pete and Leah are psyched to meet the guys. Hey, can you all be here a little early? Like six-fifteen? The guys will be going on at seven a.m. so that will give everyone plenty of time to settle in, meet the hosts, etcetera."

"Sure thing, Daniel. See you then."

I was *back*.

Forget my poor judgment of the evening before. I was a fucking good PR pro, and it was time for these guys to see me in action.

I was going to blow them away with my ability to turn the tables on their crappy image. The world would soon be eating out of their hand again, and they'd be eating out of mine.

I continued moving down my to-do list, which included setting up a Christmas USO tour and a charity concert back in LA.

But it occurred to me a Christmas tour might not be a good idea. What if they expected me to travel with them again? There was no way in hell I was going to repeat my current experience, much less over the holidays to someplace far away and war torn.

If it came to that, I'd just say no. Put my foot down. Claim I had other plans.

That I needed a kidney transplant.

I wasn't going to spend any more time than I absolutely had to with Dirty Bandit, or listening to their music.

I pulled on my noise-cancelling headphones as someone turned the music up.

## 26

# HUGH

Coral, looking cute as hell in a little purple dress, jumped out of her chair to usher in the famous Four Seasons room service. She directed them to place the shit ton of food she'd ordered on top of the credenza in the suite I was sharing with the guys.

"Jesus, Coral. Did you order every damn thing on the breakfast menu?" Stone asked, looking over the spread.

She flipped through her notebook without looking up. "Just about. I didn't know what you guys liked."

Guess she was still pissed at Ennis and me.

I kind of couldn't blame her. I mean, the girl was embarrassed. She wasn't used to how we did things. I wasn't sorry I'd watched though. That memory was going to serve me well for a long time to come.

The way she'd writhed under Ennis's mouth, her legs spread wide as she ground her pussy up in his face... my only regret was getting busted.

At the Philadelphia concert the night before, she'd given us the serious cold shoulder. She was all business and nothing more, which was bizarre because our shows were such parties, full of sweaty pleasure. We guys would have a kick-ass time on stage, getting the audience all riled up with an explosive opening song. We gave them what they wanted, egged on by the deafening rowdiness of a stadium crowd, which is part of the reason why we'd made it so big. They'd scream, stamp their feet, and sometimes even throw shit to demonstrate their fandom. Afterwards, we'd blow off steam backstage, which would be full of the hot babes the roadies rounded up, and shitloads of flowing alcohol. Drink and fuck. Fuck and drink.

It was beyond comprehension that we got paid to do this. Write music, perform to people who loved it, and then party our asses off.

I was a lucky bastard and I knew it.

But last night's after-party antics were scaled back, what with Bryan breathing down our necks. And to be honest, I didn't mind, although you'd think someone had asked Stone and Ennis for their right arms, what with all their protests.

The after-show partying was getting old. It was

strange how you could be surrounded by people talking your ear off, and yet still feel lonely.

This time, the roadies had admitted a couple girls, far fewer than the usual dozen or so they'd round up. But I, for one, just didn't feel like chatting them up. I settled into a chair, had a couple fingers of scotch, and watched our shit get packed until Stone and Ennis were ready to hit the road.

Coral had been sitting on the opposite side of the backstage area on a small loveseat the entire night, glued to her phone. I decided she'd had enough time to sulk.

"Hey, Coral?" I asked, approaching her.

If I didn't know any better, I'd swear she didn't like our music.

She looked up at me and without a word gave me one of those 'yes?' expressions.

"Why'd you wear those all night?"

The light was dim backstage, but I watched her face turn pink. She pointed to the headphones around her neck, as if I were asking about someone else's. "Oh. These? Just wanted to protect my ears. You know."

She went back to her phone.

But I wasn't giving up. "But Coral, those are *noise canceling* headphones. You weren't just protecting your ears. You didn't hear any of the concert."

Such a shame to not let go to the music. I knew she had it in her, I'd seen her let go with Ennis between her legs...

She looked up at me and shrugged. "I could hear... a little of it."

How could someone work for a rock band and not be into their music?

"Can I take this seat next to you?" I asked, joining her without waiting for an answer.

She still didn't look up from her phone. Christ, she could hold a grudge.

"Can I talk to you, Coral?" I asked.

She put the phone down. Victory. "Yes?" she said in a dull voice, her eyes cold and pissed-off.

I took a deep breath. "I'm sorry about last night in the bus. I shouldn't have invaded your privacy. I live in this little pretend world and sometimes forget that people play by different rules than we guys do. Not that that's an excuse."

She pressed her lips together and looked down, twiddling the backstage badge hanging around her neck. I was dying to slide the wall of red hair obscuring her pretty face out of the way, but I was pretty sure that would be a nonstarter.

"Whatever," she said, shrugging. "I shouldn't have been doing... that with Ennis, anyway. I'm here to work. Not have fun."

Jesus, if this woman didn't look at me I was going to lose my mind. So, I did something about it.

I put my hand under her chin with the lightest touch and turned her to me in a slow movement. If she wanted to pull away or tell me to fuck off, I wanted to give her that option.

Although, I was hoping she wouldn't.

In the dim light, her eyes looked like giant pools.

"God, you're stunning," I said.

She stiffened, her lips parted slightly.

I could practically hear what was running through her brain.

*Don't do it.*

*Stop now.*

But whatever it was, she sure as hell ignored it.

Holding her pretty face, I pulled her to me slowly, much more gently than the time I'd kissed her in front of the restaurant, when I knew I had only a moment to throw her off with my brazenness.

I touched my lips to hers. At first, she didn't respond but when I put my hand on the back of her neck and pulled her closer, she kissed me back with the passion I'd seen her exhibit the night before with Ennis.

And it was goddamn hot.

I pulled back and brushed her hair away from her face.

"It's okay," she said.

"What is?"

"That you watched. I was just embarrassed. Actually, ashamed that I'd gotten caught." She bit her lip and lowered her eyes.

"You're a beautiful woman, Coral. I know you don't think you are, but you're really what every man wants."

Her head snapped up and she looked at me like I was crazy. "I don't know about that, Hugh."

I threw my hands up. "I know what men want. I'm telling you, I know."

She took my hand off her face, and squeezed my fingers. "Thank you," she said. "You're beautiful, too."

I pressed another kiss to her mouth and looked around. We were the only ones left backstage.

"Hey, everybody's gone," I said.

She jumped to her feet in a panic. "Holy shit. Do you think they left us? C'mon," she said, grabbing my hand and pulling me to the door.

When I stopped laughing, I grabbed Coral and pulled her to me. "They can't leave without us. We're the band."

## 27

### HUGH

Stone grabbed a plate and began to pile it high with the breakfast food. When Bryan got a load of what Coral had ordered, he'd have a heart attack. He acted like we were still playing dive bars for fifty dollars and had to steal food from the kitchen when no one was looking.

But it was good to have a penny pincher around. God knew Stone, Ennis, and I didn't care how much things cost.

I had stopped worrying about money with my first royalty check from the record label. It was a crazier feeling than even when our songs began making it to the top of the charts.

Shit started getting real.

For the first time in my life, I had money, an entirely new sensation because my family hadn't had a pot to piss in when I was growing up. Hell, I'd still been sneaking into movie theaters until just one week before the money started pouring in, that's how broke I was.

By the time I could buy myself a movie ticket, I could have bought one for everyone else in line, too, if not purchased the whole damn theater if I'd wanted.

Ever hear stories about people whose lives change overnight? Yeah, it was kind of like that. But I wasn't going to be a loser about it. I paid some bills, bought an expensive pair of new sneakers, and put the rest in the bank. I wasn't going back to being broke. No fucking way.

If there was one thing I knew about rock 'n roll, it was that you could be on top one day, and it could be all over the next. If that day ever came for me, I'd be ready. I had my own house down the street from Ennis's. It might not be as big or fancy as his, but it was paid off in full and would be mine forever.

That kind of security was the best thing about Dirty Bandit's success. For me, anyway.

Not so much Stone and Ennis. They spent their money as fast as it came in. Beach houses, cars, private planes—money oozed through their fingers like water in a rushing stream.

Dealing with the kind of money we were making wasn't easy. I'd thought I could just put it in the bank and forget about it. But no, there were lawyers and accountants all looking to get their cut in exchange for the various services they offered that someone like me 'supposedly' couldn't live without.

Then there was the guilt. Nothing complicated about that. It was right beside me all the time, like a best friend.

A best friend I didn't choose. But that's just the way it was.

I'd left a shitty family situation behind me. They thought I didn't deserve my success, even though I'd worked my ass off for it. You'd think at some point I'd try to forget about them. They didn't give a shit about me, so why was I spending my time thinking about them?

If only it were that easy.

When you grow up in a situation like I did, you never completely escape the self-doubts pounded into your head from day one. They become part of you like an ugly scar that just won't fade.

I did my best not to look back. But every now and then, old memories sneaked up behind me and bit me in the ass.

*Hey, I'm over here! Don't forget me!*

When that happened, I'd run my finger over the old lump on my collarbone from a poorly healed break. My dad had thrown me against a wall because he didn't like how I was looking at him.

Or I'd run my tongue over the chipped molar from

when he'd punched me and broken a tooth that never got fixed.

Ennis took a seat next to me on the sofa, already having piled a plate high with eggs, sausage, and buttermilk biscuits. "I'm freaking starving. Good work, Coral."

He'd always been the big eater of the group. It's why they got him trainers—so he wouldn't go back to being the roly-poly kid he used to be. They told him it was for his insomnia, but no one was fooled, least of all him.

Coral paced the room with a cup of coffee in her hand, not even looking at the food. It was funny to see her worked up. I guessed the pressure was on her like it was on us right before we went onstage. It probably wasn't easy to line up a morning talk show for a bunch of semi-derelict rockers. She had a lot riding on us doing well.

She knew that once we were onstage in front of the morning's live audience, nothing she could do would us help at that point. We'd be on our own to either rock it, or fuck it up.

I didn't blame her for being worried. She knew us.

She looked at the time on her phone. "Okay guys, we're leaving in ten. Hugh, hurry, would you? And where's Bryan?"

Damn. It was all I could do not to tell her that *she* was what I'd really like to eat. She sure had liked my kiss the night before after the concert, and she'd even fallen asleep on the bus with her head on my shoulder on the short drive up to New York from Philly. But as soon as we got to the hotel, she went straight to her room, which was adjoined with ours—with the common door, of course, locked up tight.

I gave her a slow wink. "Can I get you some more coffee, Coral? With cream?"

Ennis's gaze shot up from his eggs, and he looked from Coral to me and back.

A wave of pink washed over her face so bright it nearly matched her red hair. But she shook it off.

"I'm good, Hugh," she said, tilting her head and putting her hands on her hips while throwing me a massive stink eye.

*Okay*. She could dish it out as well as take it.

My kind of woman.

"I'll eat later," I said, putting my plate down. "Hunger makes the meal all the more worth it."

She rolled her eyes.

"Cor, so what kind of dumb ass questions are these people going to be asking us, anyway?" Stone asked, shoveling the last of his pancakes in his mouth.

From the scowl on her face, she wasn't a fan of nicknames.

"They'll ask stuff about how you got started, practicing in your parents' garage, and what it's been like to rocket to stardom. They may ask a couple personal questions like whether you have girlfriends or other family," she said.

"Ugh," Stone groaned. "I hate that shit. I hate those cornball shows, and I hate that I'm about to go on one."

I waited for Coral to blow her top, but she didn't.

"I don't blame you. But maybe you should have thought of that before you got in a fight and ended up in jail."

That shut Stone right up.

She took a seat facing us. "Look, guys. No one wants to do these shows. Or if they do, they ought to have their heads examined. But this will give you the chance to show you're nice, normal, smart people." She stood to leave.

Ennis sat back in his chair, rubbing his stomach. "Holy shit that was good. I'm stuffed."

Then, Bryan wandered in. For once, he didn't have his dog.

"Christ. Who the hell ordered all this food?" he asked, grabbing a biscuit.

Ennis and I looked at each other and just smiled, ignoring him.

We headed for the door, and I sidled up to Coral. "Hey, why don't you have dinner with us tonight? Something low key, since we shouldn't go crazy partying."

She tilted her head, considering me. "That might be nice—"

"What the fuck, Hugh? Are you turning into my grandmother?" Stone burst out, bounding to his feet. "We're in the fucking Big Apple! We're not staying in our goddamn hotel room. I don't care if it is the Four Seasons. We need to *party*."

Ennis wrinkled his nose. "I don't know, Stone. I think it might be best to lay low. Not sure I'm down with lighting up the town."

Stone's eyes grew wide. "Jesus Christ, you're both a couple old ladies. I mean, what happened to my friends?" he ranted.

"Stone, can't you ever scale it back a notch? Does everything have to be a hundred miles an hour?" I asked.

Arms crossed, he glared at us. He'd be like that for the better part of the day or until he got a drink— whichever came first.

"Dude, it's not forever. We just gotta lay low for a little while to convince the label we're behaving. They'll see us redeem ourselves and then we can do whatever the hell we want," I added.

Ennis laughed. "Yeah, until we blow it again."

"How can a band that fills stadium after stadium be any sort of bad bet? We're a fucking goldmine. They'd be the fools of the century if they cut us loose."

He was right. Talk about cutting off your nose to spite your face. We were a veritable fire hose of money for those grubby bastards, and they still thought they could threaten us. It made no sense.

But if they wanted us to go on a morning talk show and wow the fans of Good Day New York, so be it.

I was more interested in making Coral's life easier. I had a feeling that might pay off in more ways than one.

She'd been mostly quiet during Stone's tantrum, letting Ennis and me play the bad cop for a change. And she'd been smart to do that. We were pretty much the only people Stone listened to.

"All right, guys. Time to go," she said, smoothing out her dress for about the hundredth time.

The *snug* dress that showed off her curvy ass and perky tits. I made sure to walk behind her to enjoy the slight jiggle of her ass cheeks under it.

Just as we were nearing the door, Stone's phone rang. He looked at its screen, turned around, and walked back to our room.

"Where the hell is he going?" Bryan asked, looking after him, looking at his watch.

"Let's go down to the car. He can meet us," Coral said, pressing the button for *lobby*.

When we got to the shiny black Town Car in front of the Four Seasons, the driver pulled open the back door. Coral slipped in, with Ennis right behind her.

I, however, walked around to the other side of the car, and got in the backseat from the driver side, putting Coral smack between Ennis and me while we waited for Stone.

It was as close to her as I'd been since the night before when she'd dozed off on the bus, and damn if she didn't smell delicious—just nice, clean girl.

Bryan leaned in the window. "Why don't you guys go ahead? I'll wait for Stone and we'll grab a taxi."

The driver raised the windows and pulled into traffic.

With Coral in such close quarters, it was all I could do to keep from staring at her legs, exposed because her dress had ridden up on her thighs. I glanced over at Ennis and found he was discreetly checking her out, too.

Coral, fortunately, was oblivious, texting Stone to hurry up.

The downy hairs on her thighs were calling my name. God, I was dying to touch her, and as the driver maneuvered in and out of Manhattan traffic, I nearly got to.

But there'd be time for that later.

## 28

## CORAL

Boob sweat was the worst.

As soon as we arrived at the Good Day New York studios and the guys were settled into a guest dressing room to wait for Stone and Bryan, I ran for the ladies' to mop myself up.

I'd ridden all the way across town in the car the studio had sent for us, squashed between Hugh and Ennis. I'd done my best to keep my nose buried in my phone, ignoring the heat surrounding me. But it was hard to concentrate so close to those two beautiful guys, one of whom I'd kissed the night before. And then fallen asleep on his shoulder.

Damn them.

If I'd known Bryan and Stone were catching their own ride, I could have hopped in the front seat. But I'd been trapped.

Was that another plan of theirs?

I'd told myself there'd be no more messing around with any of them. It was unprofessional. Unwise. Nothing good could come from it. Sure, it felt great to have Ennis's tongue lapping me between my legs, and god knew I'd fantasized about it every night since.

My decision to keep things professional lasted all of about twenty-four hours, when I'd found myself kissing Hugh backstage after the concert. Jesus, what was wrong with me? They were going to see me as nothing more than another groupie, reinforcing their already-inflated egos.

Then why did it turn me on so much to know that they couldn't keep their eyes off me at breakfast, had their gazes glued to my ass as we walked out of the hotel, and couldn't help but peek down my dress as I climbed out of this morning's car?

I dabbed myself dry with the bathroom's coarse paper towels and hustled back to the dressing room. As much as I was attracted to the guys, I didn't trust them as far as I could throw them. I dare not leave them for too long.

Stone and Bryan had arrived, thank goodness, although Stone had some kind of bug up his ass, pacing the room with a scowl that would scare off a hungry grizzly.

Stone, please don't fuck this up.

Was he still pissed by Hugh's suggestion that they spend a low-key evening together? Was it really that much of a drag for him to miss a night of partying?

But there was something else going on. No one could pout this long about a spoiled night out—not even Stone.

Whatever call he'd taken when he had to return to the room for privacy suggested that all was not well.

"Stone, are you gonna tell us what's going on?" Ennis asked.

When he provided no answer, Hugh chimed in. "Dude, what's going on? Who the hell was on the phone that set you off so bad?"

He responded with dirty looks and continued pacing and huffing.

I just hoped he could paint on a smile for the duration of his quick appearance on the show without losing his shit, and that I could get them all out of there before anyone or anything blew up.

"So guys, you ready?" I asked, cheerfully. "You're on in five."

Hugh and Ennis jumped to their feet and high-fived each other. Stone, however, just stared at the floor.

"Stone, man, can you liven up?" Ennis asked.

No answer.

"Stone, what happened? What set you off?" I dared ask.

I knew I was pushing my luck. If he were being a

dick to the guys, there was no way he'd be nice to me, but I had to get him out on that stage. Both our jobs depended on it.

He took a deep breath and looked up. "I'm fine. Let's do this. Get it over with," he said with a grimace.

*Yes.*

Doing my job—and helping the guys with their images—shouldn't be like pulling teeth. How many other times would there be when I had to beg them to do things that they would only benefit from? It made no sense.

But a lot of things about the guys made no sense to me. Like Hugh watching.

Even though it had been kind of hot.

I was pissed, and yeah, I'd run off like a frightened animal. But after I got over my initial embarrassment, all I could think about was the look on Hugh's face as he watched Ennis and me.

And what did Ennis mean that they 'liked to share'?

I followed the guys to the stage, which they entered to roaring applause. In my spot out of view of the audience, I could watch and hear everything. The guys were now live on-air, and anything they did was out of my hands.

Ennis and Hugh smiled for the screaming audience, and when they turned to the hosts, they graciously hug-kissed Leah and shook hands with Pete. Hugh stepped aside so Stone had no choice but to do the same, and he turned and waved at the audience, which went wild.

They loved him.

And I was thrilled. Whatever bug he'd had up his ass seemed gone, at least for the moment.

"Dirty Bandit, welcome to Good Day New York!" Leah chirped.

The guys smiled and nodded and proceeded to politely answer a slew of inane questions.

*Did you really start out playing in a garage?*

*Where do you get inspiration for the songs you write?*

*Did you ever think you'd get so popular?*

And on and on.

They looked so good sitting on their counter-height stools, seeming for all the world like ultra-cool rockers with their crossed legs and relaxed smiles.

It was no wonder I'd dreamed about the bastards every freaking night.

The audience was eating it up, and preliminary numbers showed a huge at-home viewership, according to one of the producers.

I looked over my shoulder to find Bryan practically dancing a jig.

The network had advertised the shit out of the show, knowing Dirty Bandit would be a big draw.

Success all around.

My phone vibrated with a text from Randall. Geez, it was four a.m. in Los Angeles.

*you're up?*

*of course. i have to watch my clients!*

*they're doing great*

*they are. i appreciate all your work. call me later. going back to bed*

The guys had been on for ten minutes so far. It was time for the hosts to wrap things up and cut to commercial.

Then why was Leah giggling maniacally and rubbing Stone's arm?

## 29

## CORAL

"Okay Dirty Bandit. One last thing before you go. Oh, by the way, can I get tickets to your next show?"

She dropped her head back and emitted that crazy laugh again. How did people watch this day after day?

Before they could answer, she continued. "Just before you came on this morning—" she slowly looked at each guy before settling on Stone, "—we got an interesting piece of news that we wanted to ask you about."

Hugh and Ennis nodded politely. Stone did not.

In fact, he looked like he was going to throw up.

Sweat trickled down his temples, and his fingers were white from gripping the arms of his chair.

What the hell was going on?

I waved at the showrunner on the other side of the stage, also out of sight of the audience, and tapped my finger on my watch.

He held up a *wait a minute* finger.

Something didn't feel right.

Leah continued.

"Word has it from a reliable source, Stone, that you've had intimate relations with an underage girl."

I clutched the wall behind me, the coffee I'd just had perilously close to ending up on the floor at my feet. Hands shaking, I reached for my phone to see if Randall had texted. So far, nothing. Had he gone back to bed, or was he, too, shocked speechless?

What the fucking fuck?

Bryan's paper cup full of coffee splattered to the floor behind me.

After a few gasps from the studio audience and an awkward silence only made worse by both the hosts' sprayed-on smiles—who fucking smiles when you're talking about sex with underage girls?—Hugh was the first to recover.

He frowned and shook his head. "Leah, that's a very serious accusation. I can tell you it's absolutely not true. Where did you hear such garbage? What sort of *reliable source* do you have that makes it okay to say something so inaccurate and so disgusting?" he said in a steady voice.

Stone didn't move, keeping his gaze glued to Hugh. It was as if he were begging for a lifeline.

Dripping with confidence, Leah laughed lightly. "Oh heavens, you know we journalists never reveal our sources. It's just not done."

She looked at her co-host, Pete, who nodded enthusiastically, like a bobble head.

Then Hugh burst forth with exactly what I was thinking. "You call yourselves *journalists*?"

Leah's eyes widened, and the smile slithered from her face.

Hugh looked at the audience and shook his head. "These two should be ashamed of themselves, propagating a disgusting rumor that they either made up or accepted at face value from someone with an axe to grind against Dirty Bandit."

Damn. He was good. If music didn't work out for him, a career in politics could be the perfect fit.

All three guys jumped to their feet at the same time.

Leah turned to the camera like nothing had ever happened.

"Thank you, Dirty Bandit, for visiting with us today—"

But Hugh was not done. "This is not the end of your bullshit, lady. You're going to be hearing from us about your desperate attempt to boost your lousy ratings."

Pete stepped forward as if he could defuse the situation, but Ennis lunged in his direction. "Back off, asshole," he growled.

The showrunner screamed *commercial*, and the guys stormed off the stage.

I grabbed Hugh's arm. "Oh my god, I love how you handled that—"

He shook me off him. "You know what, Coral? Fuck you too. You sent us into that den of middle-America mediocrity."

Did someone just slap me across the face? Because it sure felt like it.

"*Excuse me*, Hugh—"

Stone was still shocked into silence, but Ennis was not. "No, Coral. This was a bad idea."

*I* was getting blamed for this?

Ennis looked at the guys. "C'mon. Let's get the fuck out of this dump."

"Guys, guys, wait a minute," Bryan called after them.

But they ignored him, storming toward the exit when Hugh turned around and faced us. "Are you coming? Or do you want to hang out with these douchebags?" he asked, gesturing toward the producer who was hustling in our direction.

I grabbed my bag and caught up with them, Bryan tight on my heels.

Hugh flagged down a cab—who knew where the car that brought us had gone? We sure weren't going to wait for it—and we squeezed in, this time with me grabbing the front seat. As soon as the driver entered traffic, I twisted to face the back seat.

"Stone, what was that?"

He just shook his head and looked out the window.

"Yeah, Stone, what the fuck is going on?" Ennis asked, pulling his unruly hair back into the ponytail holder he kept on his wrist.

"Seriously, Ennis? Are you seriously asking me that?" Stone growled.

Hugh held his hands up. "Okay, guys, let's stay calm. We gotta figure out what we're gonna do."

"Stone, was anything she said true? I have to know. Be honest with me. It's the only way we can fix things," I pleaded, working to keep the anger out of my voice.

His gaze back at the window, he cleared his throat. "I got a text last night that something like this might come up. And then I got a call this morning, just when we were leaving."

"*What?*" Ennis shouted. "You *knew* this might come up? And you said *nothing?*"

"It's not true," Stone said in a small voice. "And I

thought that if it wasn't true, it didn't matter what anyone said."

We were silent all the way back to the hotel until we reached the guys' suite. They didn't invite me in, so I just followed them.

Stone fell onto the sofa with his head in his hands and Ennis headed to the wet bar where he opened a bottle of scotch, looked at his watch, then put it back.

It was barely ten a.m.

"Fuck, fuck, fuck," Stone murmured, rocking back and forth.

"I could use some scotch," Bryan said, looking out the window at the Manhattan skyline.

I pulled up a chair right in front of Stone and took his hands. "Tell me the whole story. Right now."

He took a deep breath. "I got a text and then a call. No idea where either came from, but they said they knew of something terrible I'd done, and that I was going to be in big trouble. The only way to keep it quiet was to *not* go on the show Good Day New York. They gave me a date for when I supposedly did it, you know, with the girl, but it was all bullshit. When I looked at my calendar, I saw I'd been at a high-stakes poker game that night. An illegal one."

He hung his head.

I never thought I'd see Stone defeated.

"Jesus, Stone—" Bryan started.

But I cut him off. "Bryan, give me a minute."

Stone raked his fingers through his hair, agony etched across his face. It was hard to be mad at someone suffering like he was. "I told whoever it was to fuck off, and they said I'd be sorry. Guess I should have listened. They knew I couldn't talk about the poker game because it was illegal. If I said anything, the guys running it would be in big trouble. So I can't even use my alibi unless I can talk one of the guys into vouching for me."

"Who would have it out for Dirty Bandit like this? Can you think of any enemies? Rivals?" I asked.

Ennis snorted. "You know how long that list would be?"

Christ, how many people had these guys rubbed the wrong way?

"Coral, I have an idea," Hugh said urgently, taking a seat next to Stone.

"What's that?"

"Remember when we went to lunch and there was that guy trying to photograph us?"

"Yeah. The weird guy with the spray-on tan and blond tips."

I'd gotten a picture of him on my phone. I started scrolling through my photo library.

"He seems to have a bug up his ass for us. Not sure why, but he follows us everywhere in LA, and is always trying to goad us, yelling things like *who's your ugly girlfriend* and *why did your last album suck so much?*"

Oh my god. He was trying to get a rise out of the guys to make them look bad. But why?

And more importantly, how could he be stopped?

## 30

## STONE

The Good Day whatever-it-was host who laid her accusation on me was lucky she was a female. I'd been known to punch out assholes for far less.

That's how I'd ended up in jail last time. And the time before. Possibly even the time before that. I couldn't really remember any more.

With hindsight being twenty-twenty and all that bullshit, I now realized I should have told Coral and the guys someone was trying to shake me down. But I just didn't think that cornball TV show, which I'd never even heard of, would announce something so messed up, especially when they had to know whoever they were getting their info from was a lying scumbag.

My bad. I assumed they cared about telling the truth. Lesson learned.

I guess for a brief moment in time, I'd mistakenly thought people would do the right thing. You know, like if they were told something terrible about someone, they might take the extra step to verify their source.

Because if they had, they'd know there was no fucking chance I'd done what I'd been accused of.

But that didn't matter. I might prove the accusation was a lie—and I planned to do just that first chance I got—but people would always attach it to my name. It was like they were compelled to enjoy remembering the worst about someone. Whether it was the truth or not had absolutely no bearing.

I just didn't get it.

It was as if there were a fucking black cloud hanging over my head that I couldn't get away from. I knew I was a lucky son of a bitch with the success of the band and all that. Was Dirty Bandit's music that much better than everyone else's out there? Hell no. We just got a few timely breaks and things had gone our way.

They might just as easily have *not* gone our way, too. Life was like that. We were surrounded by more random shit than any of us liked to believe.

I'd had my share of hard knocks in the last year or so. Some were my fault. Some weren't. But they did have me wondering if my luck was starting to run out. Like the universe only gave you so much, and when you'd exhausted your allotment, you could go suck an egg. Game over.

I left Coral and the guys and went to my room in the suite. I needed some time alone to process the shit show that had just rained down on my head as well as the consequences—there would be many—that would result.

One of the craziest and most unexpected things was that as soon as the host had dropped her bomb, I'd looked over at Coral to see her impression.

What would she think? And what would she think of me?

Obviously, I didn't expect to be her favorite human on the face of the planet. I doubted I was anyone's favorite human—I knew I was an annoying asshole. But I respected Coral and hoped she did me in return.

I knew she believed I hadn't messed around with an underage girl, just like Bryan and the guys believed me. But I didn't want to look like an idiot who never had his shit together, either. It was bad enough, my occasional temper tantrums, but I preferred avoiding looking like a total loser.

Which was new for me.

Not that I ever wanted to look like a loser. It was just that I never really cared whether people thought that or not. But with Coral? Different story.

And that was fucked up. And uncomfortable. And entirely unfamiliar.

She was smart and beautiful, without a doubt, and no guy wanted to be a douche in front of a woman like that. She was honestly trying to do good things for the band even when we gave her a hard time about it. But I think what drew me to her most was the vague memory of a self-conscious girl sitting in the corner of the cafeteria with her other awkward friends, watching the rest of us navigate the social scene that was high school. It was something some kids excelled at and others failed miserably. By some stroke of luck, Ennis, Hugh, and I had figured it out. Maybe it was because we played music. Maybe it was because we all came from such messed up family situations that we had no choice but to make high school our second home.

But how we'd done it didn't matter. What did was that Coral hadn't figured it out and I now knew, years later, that she'd suffered for it.

If I hadn't had my head so far up my ass in those days, I might have picked up on it. Maybe been a little nicer to kids outside my immediate posse. Invited them to do some shit with us. But this high school kid had no such inclination. I couldn't see beyond the end of my fucking nose.

But I could now.

And I was blown away by how graceful, accomplished, and confident Coral had become. It was as if she'd traveled the whole spectrum of growing up, whereas I'd moved about an inch. I was basically the same asshole now that I was then.

And I didn't want Coral to see that.

31

STONE

I walked over to the mini-bar in my room. Not only did the suite itself have a full bar, but each individual room also offered a small selection of booze to enjoy. I yanked open the little fridge and grabbed a couple mini vodkas. Just what the doctor ordered, even if it were still morning.

I was sitting on the edge of my bed about to crack open the first bottle when there was a knock on my door.

"Yeah?"

As humbled as I was, another lecture or further admonishment was not anything I was in the mood for.

"Um, Stone, it's Coral. Can I come in?"

"Oh. Sure."

My door opened slowly, and she poked her head in, looking around for me in the dim light of my room where I'd closed all the black-out drapery. When she spotted me on the bed, she entered the rest of the way.

As much as I was grateful to have her around, there was a piece of me wondering if she were somehow responsible for arranging the mess we ended up in.

But that was the old me, looking for someone else to blame for my troubles. She'd only tried to do her best by us guys.

"I wanted to talk to you about your alibi—the party you were at on the night you were accused."

Of course she wanted to talk about that. Everyone wanted to talk about that. Problem was, there was nothing to say.

I'd played poker with some guys that run illegal games. There weren't a lot of high stakes choices out there, and sometimes if you really wanted to play, your only choice was one where the house took a "stake," meaning they took part of the monies bet during the game.

I didn't care if they took a cut, as long as I got my gambling itch scratched.

But the problem was that the games were top secret, so secret that if you blabbed about them, you'd never get to play again.

So getting them to vouch for me was almost impossible. They weren't going public, no fucking way.

They'd laugh their asses off if I even asked—they didn't care what the hell I'd been accused of.

"If you can't disclose where you were that night, we need to take another approach." She scrolled through her phone. "Have you seen this guy before?"

Oh. Shit.

I nodded. "Yup. I might have shoved him one night."

Realization washed over her face. Or was it relief?

"Shoved him? What does that mean?" she asked.

I took a deep breath. "I might have shoved him, like in the face."

She sighed. "Okay. Thank god I have the photo. I'm going to send it to my boss in LA and get him working on ID'ing the guy."

She put her hand on my arm and damn if it didn't feel fucking awesome, considering the day I'd had. "I'm going to my room to make some calls. But let's all get together for dinner tonight. I think we need to do something nice for ourselves."

I could think of a couple nice things she could do for me. But first, I wanted to do something nice for her.

I couldn't wait to get the hell out of New York. I'd never liked the place, with its people so dripping with ambition they didn't care who they stepped over on the way up. I was usually good for one or two nights of partying in the Big Apple, and then I was done.

And that day, I was seriously *done*. Shit, Bryan had caught the first flight back to LA that he could. Something about meeting with the label and being there in person for it.

Better him than me. I always managed to piss them off with my big mouth.

After Coral had left my room, I'd fallen into what I called one of my twenty-minute *stress naps*. I'd always been a big sleeper, and when the going got rough, it was where I retreated to. Some might say it was a cop out, but on more than one occasion it had kept me from punching someone's lights out—and from the free night in county jail that often followed.

My mini-snooze helped to reset my mood. The strange thing about today's nap, though, was that I dreamt of Coral the whole time.

She was getting under my skin. And she wasn't even trying.

God, I was turning into a pussy.

But I'd made sure I got to sit right next to her at the trendy Chelsea restaurant we went to for dinner.

As usual, heads turned when we came in and a couple folks even whistled to get our attention. But we just waved, kept our heads down, and were seated in a far corner of the restaurant where we could have peace and quiet.

I grabbed Coral's hand under the table. The other guys might have seen, but I didn't give a shit. They'd be cool with it.

And to my delight, she didn't pull away. In fact, she gripped my fingers right back.

## 32

## CORAL

When we'd gotten back from dinner, Ennis invited me to the guys' suite for a drink.

I knew what that meant.

And I was tempted, truth be told. I didn't know exactly what they had in mind, but I trusted them enough to know they didn't want to do anything I didn't want to do.

But, I made my excuses. "Thanks, Ennis. I need some time to myself. I'm getting in bed with a book."

And we said our good nights.

Next morning, Hugh knocked on our adjoining door.

"Pack your stuff," he said when I opened it.

I frowned, looking at my clothes strewn all over the room. "Huh?"

I wasn't ready to go anywhere. I was all cozy in my yoga pants and an oversized sweatshirt, tapping away on my laptop, and really wasn't interested in moving.

He walked into my room and looked around. "You don't have too much stuff. Do you need help getting it all together?"

Ennis came in right behind him.

"Hugh, what are you talking about? Why do I need to pack?" I asked.

Shit. Were they firing me? *Could* they fire me?

I grabbed my phone to see if I'd missed a call or text from Randall.

Nothing.

Well, if they *were* giving me the boot, I was going down kicking. I hadn't busted my ass just to be thrown out.

And I couldn't deny any longer that, in spite of myself, I had a bit of a crush on all three of the rascals. So I had further reason to want to stick around. Unprofessional as it might be.

"Coral, we want to get back home. Bryan chartered us a plane to LA, and we're leaving in an hour."

Holy crap. I'd never been in a private plane.

"Why? Why are we leaving now?" I asked.

Stone walked in behind the guys. He looked much better than he had the day before, freshly showered and with the bags under his eyes nearly gone. "We just want to get the hell home. Don't you?"

"Well, yeah. Okay. Oh my god, an hour?" I frantically looked at the crap all over my room. "I'll be ready. An hour is plenty of time to get ready."

Ennis laughed. "What Hugh meant to say was the plane is *leaving* in an hour. We get picked up in"—he looked at his watch—"five minutes."

"Shit!" I said, running to shove my laptop and all my papers into my tote bag.

"We're almost ready, too, so we'll be right back to help."

Oh my god. Five minutes?

I ran into the bathroom and swept everything off the counter into the hotel's plastic laundry bag. Then I grabbed everything out of my closet and off the chairs I had it draped over, stuffing it all into my suitcase.

I checked under the bed and in the dresser drawers like you're supposed to when leaving a hotel. The coast was clear.

I wiped the sweat from my brow and wheeled my bag into the guys' room, where they all stood by the door holding their duffels. Ennis hustled over and took my suitcase, and Stone grabbed my tote.

Well.

"I think that's the record for bolting out of a hotel to catch a flight," Hugh said laughing.

We jumped into the Town Car waiting at the curb,

and in thirty minutes we were boarding a private plane.

## 33

## CORAL

Holy shit. So this was how the rich lived.

"This is insane," I said, plopping into a cushy club chair after a pretty flight attendant had taken our bags.

The guys had grabbed chairs, too, which we rotated so they faced each other.

"It's like a little club house. Just for us four," I said.

The flight attendant handed each of us a glass of champagne. "I'll just be in the back, should you need anything. I'm grabbing a seat for takeoff," she said, pointing to a space beyond a curtain.

Moments later, the plane started accelerating.

"How did Bryan get this plane?" I asked, looking

around at gorgeous paneled walls, thick carpeting, and full bar.

A girl could get used to this. Especially after a freaking bus.

"Bryan worked his magic. It probably belongs to some rich person who wasn't using it. I'm sure it wasn't cheap," Ennis said, shrugging. "Guess he thought it was okay to splurge to get us back home."

As soon as the plane was in the air, I got up for the restroom. We'd left so abruptly I'd not even combed my hair, and from the wind on the tarmac, I was a mess. Maybe I was an idiot for caring how I looked. But there it was.

I was traveling with three of the most beautiful men I'd ever known, and even though they were clients, I couldn't deny that being with them made my heart race.

They might have thought I was once the homely, sad girl in the lunchroom, but I was going to ensure they knew I'd left her far, far behind.

When I slid aside the bathroom door to exit, Stone was standing right in front of it. Blocking my way.

"Oops. Excuse me, Stone."

I tried to step around him, but he didn't give way. He just stood there, smiling down on me, his feet firmly planted in front of the accordion door. And there was no way around him.

I looked up to find his gaze on my lips.

I'd thought it sweet, the way he'd held my hand

under the table at dinner the night before, as if it were his way of thanking me for listening.

And now, he took my hand again.

"You know how beautiful you are?" he whispered.

Oh my gosh. Was he going to kiss me, right here, on the plane, in the bathroom doorway? Shit, the other guys were just around the corner, and the flight attendant could appear at any moment.

But he'd been through such a rough time, and he really was a teddy bear beneath his hard rock exterior.

He got closer, and then his lips closed in on mine.

This kiss was different from the one we'd shared in the pool. That was off-hand, almost cocky. Non-committal. Showoff-y.

This one was connected. And patient. And I found my free hand wandering up around his neck.

"Daaaaamnnnn," someone growled.

I nearly jumped out of my skin, and turned to see Hugh staring at us wearing a shit-eating grin.

Busted.

"Hugh, you do have a thing about watching, don't you?" I said, trying my best to scowl at his interruption.

But the truth was, it turned me on.

Shit.

The intensity of the last few days—the awkwardness of the bus ride, the high of getting the guys on the talk show, the devastation of having the host drop her little bomb, to name a few—had been almost more than

I could take. This damn job was taking years off my life.

And as hard as it had been for me, I knew it was multiples harder for the guys.

Maybe this was our way of letting off steam?

As Hugh approached me, Stone loosened his hold on the back of my neck.

"I do like to watch, Coral. But I also like to join in," he said.

I looked nervously at Stone.

But a smile spread over his face, and he stepped aside for his friend.

Holy shit.

Hugh placed his hand on the back of my head and grabbed a fistful of my hair.

Oh god.

I gasped from the fierceness of it, and resisted against the strange angle he'd pulled me into.

"Hugh, what are you—"

But his mouth was on mine before he could finish, equally as delicious as Stone's kiss but completely different at the same time. It was rougher. Almost crude. And definitely demanding.

So different from the other night, when it seemed like he was just feeling me out.

And I was still standing in the doorway of the goddamn airplane bathroom, with the flight attendant passing by, not even looking in our direction.

Did rich people with private planes do this all the time?

I couldn't blame them. It was kind of fun.

Hugh suddenly stepped back from our kiss, wearing a wicked little smile.

I'd show him, leaving me standing there, gaping like a fish with my mouth open from his hot kiss. I just acted normal—like I sucked face with hot rock stars all the time. On private jets, of course.

So I smoothed out my hair and adjusted my shirt, leaning against the doorway to still my shaking knees.

"Hey, fuckers. What about me?" Ennis asked.

Oh my god. Did he want to kiss me, too?

I sure as hell hoped so.

So I stepped out of the restroom and leaned against the galley wall. Without hesitation, Ennis walked right up to me and ran his lips down the side of my neck. My eyes fluttered closed, and even though I was trying to play it cool, a small moan escaped my mouth.

His kiss sent me to another world, one where I couldn't think. Which was fine. Perfect, really. All I wanted was to feel.

He took my hand and placed it on his hard cock. "Stroke me, baby," he murmured, finding my breasts and kneading me almost to the point of pain.

*Almost.*

"That is fucking *hot*," Stone snarled.

I looked at the other guys from the corner of my

eye. They stood there, arms crossed, smiling, and very much enjoying the show.

But not as much as I was enjoying it.

Even if it were confusing the hell out of me.

I brought my lips to Ennis's ear and whispered. "What's with you three guys?"

I had no desire to ruin the moment, but having an audience, coupled with his erotic touching, brought me close to losing my mind.

And I loved it. Maybe too much.

He pulled back to look at me. "We *share*. Have you ever heard of sharing?"

Um, yeah, I'd heard of sharing. Like sharing a pizza. Or sharing a ride.

Not sharing a woman.

He saw the confusion cross my face. "We'd like to share you, Coral."

I stepped away from him, looking at the other guys.

"Is this some kinky rock 'n roll thing?"

Ennis burst out laughing. "No, beautiful. Although we are kinky. And we are rock 'n roll. Now if you'll just relax and enjoy the flight, you'd see what we mean."

Hugh walked toward me and took my hand. "I'd like to continue what we started the other night."

Holy shit. I looked around. The curtain was drawn across the galley, and the flight attendant was nowhere in sight.

"Why don't you undress?" Ennis asked in a quiet voice.

Although it was more of a command than request.

And what did he mean, anyway? Undress right there? In the airplane?

I looked from one guy to the other. They smiled and nodded.

"Only if you want to, of course," Hugh added.

Undress for three of the most gorgeous men I'd ever laid eyes on?

Who, incidentally, I'd gone to high school with?

And who were also my firm's biggest clients?

So many reasons to say no.

And only one reason to say yes.

## 34

CORAL

Every inch of my being screamed *go for it*. There was just no drowning it out.

These guys were inches from getting dropped by their record label. And if that happened, my firm would be next on the chopping block, only to be followed by my employment. Or lack thereof.

So, fuck it.

I lifted my shirt, then peeled down my yoga pants, kicking the whole mess to the floor. There I stood, in my lacy pink bra and matching thong.

Thank god I was wearing cute undies and not the granny panties I'd been known to save for travel. If there had been more time before we left the hotel, I very likely would have ended up changing into those ugly things. I mean, I didn't usually get on a plane thinking I was going to be undressing at some point.

But there was a first for everything.

Once mostly naked, I wasn't sure what to do next. But I didn't have to worry because it seemed like the guys knew just what to do. Two hands landed on my ass, kneading handfuls of my generous flesh. A quick look over my shoulder confirmed it was Stone, who ground his hard cock against me and nuzzled my hair. While I let my head fall back on his chest, Ennis took up residence before me, lowering my bra straps and caressing my now-hard nipples.

Not about to be left out, Hugh reached inside my thong. "Fuck, baby. You're soaking wet."

I closed my eyes and sank into the sensation of three pairs of hands working the most sensitive parts of my body. Their movements, and the occasional rocking of the plane, lulled me into a space of pure, primal sensuality where my breath came rough and raspy, their fingers moving me toward an explosion that would hit me like a truck.

In the back of my mind, I knew I shouldn't have been messing around with the guys, but there was no fucking way anything was stopping us now. It just felt too goddamn good, being worshipped by three gorgeous men who, if I were honest with myself, I had more in common with than I'd ever dreamed. They weren't the evil creatures I'd thought they were in high school, just like I wasn't the clueless nerd they'd assumed I was.

Not that any of that mattered now.

I reached inside someone's jeans—whose, I wasn't even sure—and grabbed a hard cock that was wet at the very tip. As the guys went to town on my ass, clit, and tits, I stroked the cock down to the balls and back up to its swollen head.

"Yeah baby, work my dick like that," Ennis whispered, pushing himself further into my hand.

My eyes fluttered open and I was face to face with his beautiful smile and dimples. The sensation of being taken by all three guys filled me with some kind of animal hunger I didn't know I possessed. I opened Ennis's jeans all the way for complete access to his dick, and in one swift movement, I pushed the other guys away so I could fall to my knees and take him in my mouth.

While I did, I parted my legs so the guys could reach my pussy.

With my hands gripping his ass cheeks, I took Ennis until he hit the back of my throat. With my other hand I gently pulled and twisted his balls, causing him to howl such that he was probably heard all the way up in the cockpit.

"Fuck, baby," he hollered, "I'm gonna come in your mouth."

He grabbed my head and with fistfuls of my hair, slammed me down on his cock. Just when I thought he couldn't get any bigger, he lengthened one last time in my mouth before he filled me with his semen.

I couldn't take it fast enough. I sputtered while the extra ran down my chin and onto my tits.

When I'd milked him of his last drop, he helped me to my feet. Turning toward Stone and Hugh, I looked from one to the other.

"I want you to fuck me. Now," I whispered, wondering who would accept my invitation.

The guys looked at each other as if they shared some sort of wordless language. Stone nodded, and Hugh smiled. It was clear Hugh was the appointed one as he reached into his pocket and retrieve a condom. Weaving his fingers into mine, he brought me back to the cushy club chairs where we'd been earlier. He took a seat and positioned me right in front of him. Opening his pants, he sheathed himself with the condom.

He looked at me the way he had the other night after the concert, when I admitted to myself how damn good his dominance felt. Such comfort. And protection.

Things I never knew I wanted. And now they were coming to me from the least likely place.

"You wanna ride me, beautiful?"

As if he needed to ask. I'd never wanted something this much, his cock so deep inside me I could feel it up in my throat.

With the other guys watching, of course.

I looked over my shoulder to make sure they were

there, and caught both smiling. Stone nodded at me. "Do it baby. I want to see you get fucked."

Well, that was all I needed. I placed my knees on either side of Hugh's hips and grabbed the chair back for purchase. He reached under me, holding his cock firm.

I lowered myself just until he touched my opening. Our gazes locked intimately as I rubbed my wet pussy over him.

"You teasing me, baby?" he growled.

Triumphant, I looked at him. "Maybe."

"Open yourself. I want to be inside," he demanded.

Well, then.

I reached between my legs and parted my lips just a bit. Lowering myself, I allowed him to slide between my fingers where I held myself open.

"Are you being selfish with your pussy?" he asked with a smile.

"Fuck her, dude. C'mon," a voice behind me said.

I looked over my shoulder and saw that Ennis had taken a seat. Stone stood, shoulders hunched, as edgy as I'd ever seen him.

"You guys are soooo impatient. As if you don't do this all the time."

Yeah, I was fishing.

Hugh tilted his head at me, the fingers of one hand curling around the back of my neck, the others kneading one of my breasts. "I know what you're thinking, that we screw every girl who looks our way. But you're not every girl. You're fucking amazing."

Alrighty then.

I slowly lowered myself until I was full of his cock, my head dropping as the intense pressure ignited a rumble in my core that I knew was going to become something explosive.

"Fuck baby, you feel good," he said, his hands sliding to my hips as he guided me up and down.

"Looks good, too," Stone said.

"Yeah?" Hugh breathed. "You guys watching our girl's pussy get fucked?"

*Our girl?*

Various grunts and groans were the response.

Hugh's cock slid in and out, hitting the elusive spot that I knew would make me explode in just a few—

"Oh god, Hugh," I said, rubbing my lips against the tattoo on his neck, "I'm coming. Fuck!"

With that, he pistoned me up and down on his cock until I was screaming so loudly the pilots probably heard me. I didn't really care.

Just when my second orgasm started to hit, I realized someone was standing on my left. I looked up to find Stone, his jeans open to his hard cock. Without a second thought, I took him in my mouth while another orgasm battered me.

With my eyes closed, I rocked from the movement of both guys fucking my pussy and mouth, and the plane hitting light turbulence. Stone started to spurt in my mouth just as Hugh gripped my hips and pulled me down tight, nearly to his balls. He pulsed inside me as I rubbed my clit for one last orgasm.

"Fuck, baby," Stone said, slowly withdrawing from my mouth. "Jesus guys, she swallowed all I had to give her."

I dreamily opened my eyes, pushing hair off my sweaty face. "I hope that's not all you have to give."

## 35

ENNIS

"Do you think she's ever done anything like that before?"

I frowned at Stone. He could be such an idiot. "Hell no."

He looked at his watch to make sure she wasn't coming up the walkway to the house. "What a little honey. Man, the way she sucked your dick and then rode Hugh—"

"Morning guys," Coral said, flying through my front door.

I could be flattering myself—god knew I'd done that before—but I could swear there was a little spring in her step that morning. Of course, I wanted to believe it was from the proposal we'd made to her. And the fun we'd had on the plane.

When our flight landed and we were in the limo on the way home, a sadness washed over me knowing she was going to her home, and we to ours. I didn't want to say goodnight.

But I wasn't going to tell her that. And it turned out I didn't need to. Guess I had it written all over my sappy fucking face.

"I'll be over, first thing in the morning," Coral had promised, tangling her fingers in my hair and pulling me in for a goodnight kiss.

And now our girl was back.

Shit. Ever since Hugh had said *our girl*, I couldn't stop thinking of her that way.

"Hey, beautiful," Hugh said, kissing the top of her head and handing her a cup of coffee.

"Dude. Where's *my* coffee?" Stone asked.

"In the kitchen, asshole."

I burst out laughing. Couldn't help it. Stone was an awesome guy, but he stepped into it all the time with his big damn mouth.

Coral's head dropped back with the laugh that had captivated me the first time we met—back when we were resisting her with all our might.

As dickish as we'd been early on, she'd never been deterred. Sure, she walked out the door that one time, not giving a shit what happened to Dirty Bandit, but she knew all along we needed her and that we'd always come running back.

Never thought I'd see the day when we desired someone so much. And I didn't mean just her PR services.

"Okay, guys," she said, pulling a notebook out of her bag, and smiling as we each took note of the strappy dress that showed off her beautiful shoulders.

"The limo picks us up in fifteen. Let's go over today's event one more time. Our first Arianna's Pantry fundraiser, named after Ennis's sister, is being held at The Grove. Dirty Bandit will play a short show for an admission of twenty dollars per head plus one can of donated food. We'll get there, do a press conference, warm up with the rest of the band, and be back home in time for dinner."

Even while my breath hitched at the mention of my little sister's name, I wondered what had we done all these years without Coral. Bryan had tried to set up promos for us from time to time, but he wasn't a details guy and so many things always went wrong that each time we vowed never to do one again.

No wonder we'd earned ourselves such a shitty reputation.

After a brief on-stage rehearsal, where I was pleased to find that Coral did *not* wear her noise-canceling headphones, we sat in a trailer that had been set up as a dressing room.

"So, you give any thought to our proposal yester-day?" Hugh asked, looking directly at her.

No beating around the bush, there. Hugh was usually a little more subtle. Maybe he'd been hanging around Stone too much.

But I was dying for an answer too. I couldn't deny it.

"I... I'm still thinking about it," she said, a pink blush washing over her pretty face. "I need some time."

I nodded. Hugh was pushing it, but I also knew he was eager. We all were.

"Take your time, baby. It's not every day a bunch of rock 'n roll assholes want to share you," I said, trying to lighten things up.

Coral laughed, happy the tension was broken, and jumped to her feet. "Well. It's show time. We're starting with the press, you'll play, and then we're done. Are we good?"

We looked at each other and nodded.

Coral opened the trailer door and called to Bryan. "We're ready."

I looked past her and saw a gaggle of about twenty-five or so journalists and photographers. Just in front of the trailer was a table big enough for us three guys, and microphones for each of us.

We grabbed our seats, and Coral started, with all eyes on her. "Friends, thank you for helping spread the word about Arianna's Pantry, Dirty Bandit's new phil-anthropic foundation. We're kicking things off today with a beautiful outdoor concert here at The Grove, and we're really excited to see where it takes us."

Damn, she was good. And good-looking, with that red hair fluttering in the warm breeze. Later, when we got her home…

*Down boy.*

"Before you get started interviewing the guys, I want to address a couple bits that have been floating around the rock world regarding Dirty Bandit." She looked over at us and smiled. I had no idea where she was going with things, but it didn't matter. I trusted her.

She looked down at her hands and took a deep breath. I didn't know if it was just for effect or actually sincere, but it grabbed everyone's attention.

"The band, Dirty Bandit," she paused, looking at the three of us one-by-one, "have never been angels. They live by their own rules—for better or for worse."

A titter spread through the crowd.

She smiled. "But the story about Stone, that vicious rumor started by the Good Day New York program, is false. Completely false and invented by someone with an axe to grind."

I followed her gaze over the audience and heard her falter for a split second. But she kept right on going after a sip of her water.

She'd been looking way in the back, at the creepy photographer guy she'd told us she was concerned about. He wore a red baseball cap and a strange smirk on his orange fake-tan face. Occasionally, he picked up his camera, adjusted his super-long lens, and took a few snaps.

I nudged Stone who followed my gaze. "Red cap," I murmured.

He looked over the crowd and gave a slow nod, so discreet that not even Hugh on the other side of him noticed.

"The important thing is that today we're kicking off the foundation named after Ennis's sister, Arianna, whom he tragically lost a few years ago. Ennis, would you like to say a few words?"

Fuck. I stood, the lump building in my throat. I thought I'd be okay. Surely after all this time I could talk about Arianna without losing my shit, right?

Wrong.

## 36

## ENNIS

I cleared my throat. "Thank you, everyone, for coming today. As the guys here will tell you"—I motioned to Stone and Hugh—"losing Arianna changed everything about my life. Years later, it's still hard to talk about her." My voice broke.

Goddammit.

"I've wanted to do something to honor her for a while and was never sure what that should look like, until now. When someone suggested a foundation dedicated to one of her most passionate interests— childhood hunger, I realized I'd found the perfect project. Luckily for me, my bandmates were on board. So, thank you, Stone and Hugh, for believing in

Arianna the way I do, and Coral, another hometown girl on this journey with us, for your support, and for making this a reality."

Coral tilted her head and nodded, like the guys did.

Whew. Got that out of the way.

The usual barrage of questions came flying at all of us, but there was one designed, I had no doubt, to throw Stone off track. It didn't work.

"Stone, if you weren't with that underage girl, what were you doing that night? Can you tell us? That would certainly get you off the hook," one of the reporters asked.

Stone took the mic. "Fair question, and I've been grappling with answering that myself. You see, I was playing poker that night. Unfortunately, it was an illegal game, so I've been pretty quiet about it. For obvious reasons, I can't divulge the names of anyone else who was there."

"So basically, no one can vouch for where you were that night."

He pressed his lips together and slowly shook his head. "No one so far."

A chatty buzz spread through the group, with a couple people shaking their heads in disbelief.

Coral had been right. You do all the good things you can, and people still focus on the one negative thing, true or not.

"Okay, everybody, Dirty Bandit needs to head up to the stage now. Looks like they've got a full house.

Thank you for coming, supporting our cause, and we hope you enjoy the show," Coral said.

As soon as she'd handed the technician her mic, she shot through the slowly dispersing crowd, heading straight for the guy with the red cap. When he saw her coming his way, he picked up his pace away from the event.

But she caught up with him, anyway. And he got right in her face.

If there was one thing I hated, it was dudes who thought they could intimidate women to get them to back down.

I caught up to them, dodging several reporters' questions on the way.

"Is there a problem here?" I asked, extending my hand to the man. "I don't think I caught your name."

"You don't need to know my name," he hissed.

Yeah, there was definitely something off about this guy.

But Coral was ready for him. "His name is Carr Evanston. He and Stone had an altercation a while back. And I think he was the one to spread the rumor about Stone."

"Fuck off, bitch," he spat, and took off.

I started after him, but Coral grabbed me. "Not now, Ennis. We need to get you onstage."

As he walked out of sight, he turned several times to look back over his shoulder.

"C'mon," she said.

While we hustled toward the rest of the band, I was dying to take Coral's hand. There would be nothing appropriate about that in a public setting, especially when she was clearly our publicist and working so hard to spruce up our image, but I just wanted to touch her, however briefly.

So just before I jumped up on stage, I ran my hand over her red hair, shiny and warm from the sun.

"Thank you for helping with Arianna's Pantry. It feels really good. After a busy day like this, the guys and I would usually go party it up. I don't know what you've done to us, Coral, but that's not even on the table right now."

A shy smile spread across her face. She grabbed a couple of my fingers and gave them a quick squeeze.

"Of course, Stone's the same asshole he's always been. You can only work so many miracles."

She dropped her head back and laughed.

Hours later, on the quick drive home, I lay my head back on the seat, exhausted. "How did we used to go out and party after a day like this? All I can think about is having a drink and chilling by the pool."

The guys nodded. But Coral frowned, her gaze glued to her phone screen.

"Something up, sweetie?" Hugh asked.

She sighed deeply and popped her phone back into her purse. "Stone, do you think there's a chance you can get just one of your poker friends to vouch for you?"

He nodded slowly. "Possibly. I do think there's one guy who will do me a solid. I just gotta track him down."

She looked between the two other guys. Was she avoiding my gaze?

What the hell?

"I just got word that there's a new story hitting about the band. It's not pretty."

There were stories about the band all the time. But something about Coral's expression indicated that this was one of the less pleasant ones.

And what could be less pleasant than Stone's accusation, anyway?

Finally, her gaze settled on *me*.

"Ennis, they're saying you're using the death of your sister and launch of the foundation to improve your standing. And that the car wreck was your fault."

## 37

CORAL

Cripes. How did a day that started out so promising end up so fucked?

Oh wait. I'd had a day just like this one in New York, barely forty-eight hours ago.

I didn't know what it was with Dirty Bandit. I mean, did they have a goddamn black cloud hanging over their heads?

Or maybe this was the way it was when you were at the top. There was just no end to the people wanting to take you down.

But I had a strong feeling I knew who was behind these setbacks.

If there was one positive thing coming out of

the shit show that was Dirty Bandit's public life, it was that it was pulling the four of us closer together.

Did I just say the four of us?

I needed to have my head examined.

After we'd gotten back to Ennis's house, there was not a happy face in the room.

Stone pounded his fist on the arm of the chair where he sat. "It's like we're at the bottom of some pit trying to crawl out and some fucker just keeps dumping more dirt on top of us."

I took a seat next to Ennis and rubbed his thigh. "Don't worry. We'll take care of this."

Stone was pacing the living room, looking past the pool to the hills, where I think we all would have liked to have been hiding at the moment.

"Ennis, you know it's not your fault. Dude, you gotta shake that shit off," he said. "You know there are haters out there. We've dealt with them since day one. They'll never go away, so long as we're on top. If it's not this, it's something else."

Ennis looked down at his hands and shook his head the slightest amount.

He didn't need to say a word. I could feel his pain, and I knew what it was like to try to shake something off that would just never go away.

"I'll be fine," he said in a voice so quiet I barely heard him.

I took his hand. "I'm sorry this happened, Ennis."

Hugh walked up and crouched in front of him. "You know how this is, man. You've been through it before."

Now that I'd been around the guys for a while, I could see they really had been through a lot, both together and on their own. For all their good luck and fortune, they still had problems just like anybody else.

Ennis rose to his feet. "I'm going for a swim," he said, dropping his T-shirt on the floor as he walked. When he reached the French doors, his jeans dropped to his ankles. Stepping out of them, he kicked them aside, just like he had his workout clothes that day on the bus.

Which seemed like a year ago, but in reality had been only days.

"Great idea, man," Hugh said, running after him with Stone close behind.

Within seconds, there were three nude men in Ennis's pool. Maybe they had room for one more person?

But before I could join them, my phone rang. "Hi, Randall," I said to my boss.

"Hey, Coral. Crazy day, huh?" he said.

I guess he'd heard. I guess everybody in the world had heard, actually.

I lowered my voice. "The guys just can't seem to get a break. First Stone, then this bullshit about Ennis."

"Sounds like someone's losing their objectivity," he quipped.

What the hell was that supposed to mean?

"Randall. They're our client. Of course we are biased toward them."

I kicked off my shoes. The guys were having too much fun in the pool not to join them.

Time to wrap up my call.

"Mmmm hmm," he said quietly.

What was going on?

"I know you've worked hard on this client, Coral."

"Yes, I have. It's a great opportunity for us and the firm, right?"

At least that's what he'd told me when he first assigned the account to me. But something in his tone was off.

"Coral, I don't know whether we should continue with these guys."

Huh?

My stomach flipped and a wave of angry heat blasted across my face. *Not continue?* What the hell did that mean?

I lowered my voice. "What guys? You mean the band?"

I looked outside to make sure they were still splashing around in the pool and moved to the far side of the living room in case someone came in and heard me.

"Yeah. I mean Dirty Bandit. They have one problem after another. Serious problems. At some point it's going to reflect badly on the firm to keep a client accused of underage sex and being responsible for a car crash that killed a sister."

I sank onto a funky Mexican stool in the corner of the living room where I could see everyone coming and going.

My heart started to race, and my voice got tight. "What are you saying, Randall? That we need to release them from their contract? What is Bryan going to say? I thought he was an old buddy of yours."

"I'm afraid that's the direction we're heading in, Coral. It's going to look really bad if we have sexual offenders and drunk drivers on our client roster. It could impact my friendship with Bryan, but it's business. I suspect he'll understand that."

Holy fucking shit.

Had Randall fallen for a bunch of ugly rumors? Or did he just want to distance himself from a client he thought was beyond help?

Either way, fury washed over me.

I took a deep breath to steady myself. "How can you say that, Randall? Don't you know all that stuff is lies? It's our job to help prove that. But you want to bail? You think that would look better than a client with problems?"

I was trembling with anger.

And fear, if I were honest with myself.

I believed Dirty Bandit deserved the chance to defend themselves. And I didn't want to stop seeing them on a regular basis.

For work purposes, of course.

"We need to think of the firm, Coral," he said.

Did he need reminding that he'd told me to *think of the firm* when he'd assigned Dirty Bandit to me?

"Okay, Randall. Give me more time. If we make these guys shine the way I think we can, we'll be heroes."

"I don't know. I just don't know," he said.

"Please. Just another week, tops."

He sighed. "Okay. One week."

## 38

CORAL

So not only was the shit hitting the fan for Dirty Bandit, the PR firm might be dumping them, too.

Life was so fucking brutal. I'd had about all I could take for one day and wanted nothing more than a dip in the pool.

But something was holding me back.

I liked the guys. Probably too much.

There was Hugh, with his quiet sensitivity that contrasted wickedly with his shaved head and neck tattoo, trying to leave behind a sad family situation that just kept following him.

Stone's raw sensuality and confidence, which could

come off like a bull in a china shop, made my heart race every time he touched me.

And Ennis, constantly pushing that thick mop of hair off his gorgeous brow, staggering under the guilt of his sister's death.

What would I do without these guys? They frustrated me to no end, drove me up a wall, made me laugh, and gave me the best orgasms of my life.

I mean, how many women messed around with three hot guys who wanted to 'share' her?

I still didn't know how that shit was supposed to work.

More importantly, I wasn't sure I wanted to.

"Coral!" Stone called. "Come on in."

Oh, what the hell.

I ripped off my clothes in the middle of the living room, ran to the pool, and jumped in.

"Woo-hoo!" Stone hollered. "Coral's here!"

"Who was on the phone?" Hugh asked, treading water and trying to get a look at my boobs.

Ugh. I wasn't sure what to tell them. So I decided to tell them a version of the truth.

"It was my boss, Randall. He's concerned about all that's going on. You know, first with Stone then with Ennis."

Yeah, he was so concerned that he wanted to jump ship.

Stone climbed out of the pool and bent for a towel, his

ass muscles flexing and the late afternoon sun reflecting off his wet body. He turned to face the pool, absentmindedly rubbing the towel over his balls to dry them off.

What was it with guys and their balls?

Then, he fell onto a lounge chair and lay back, hands behind his head, closing his eyes and smiling while he dried in the sun.

And he was fucking beautiful.

"I think you like what you see," Hugh said quietly, treading water right in front of me.

Busted. I *had* been staring pretty hard

I splashed water in his direction. "So what?" I asked and then swam underwater.

When I came back up, both Hugh and Ennis were sitting on the edge of the pool with their feet in the water.

"Hey, gorgeous," Ennis called. "Why don't you come over here?"

Oh my god. They were both stroking hard-ons.

So hot. So dirty.

And I loved it.

I swam toward them, keeping a flirtatious distance. "You need something, boys?"

"Baby, my dick's been hard since I saw your tits bouncing on your way out here. Do you think you could help a guy out?"

"No, darlin', I'm the one needing help," Stone called out.

I rotated in the water to see him stroking his own erection in the lounge chair where he lay.

Holy crap. Did I need to choose? How the hell was I supposed to do that?

"I might be able to help you," I said, mesmerized by the hand stroking up and down his shaft. "All three of you," I added.

I bounced up and down in the water playfully, making sure they got a good look at my tits.

I couldn't resist these guys. I just couldn't.

I swam toward Ennis and when I reached him, gripped his thighs and lowered my mouth over his raging erection. From the corner of my eye, I could see Hugh stroking himself, and Stone doing the same on the lounge chair.

I took Ennis's cock until it banged the back of my throat. Something about the crazy day, and being in the sunshine with these three beautiful men, left me starving for some naughtiness, as if that were a way to shake off the day's crap.

"Fuck, baby, you're taking the whole thing," Ennis said, his hand on my head. "Guys, why don't you show Coral how fucking hot she is?"

I had no idea what he had in mind, and it didn't matter.

Pulling Ennis's cock out of my mouth, I ran my tongue around his head, my gaze glued to his until I noticed Stone and Hugh standing on either side of him.

Flanking him, they continued to stroke their cocks, aiming them right at me.

In the afternoon sunshine, I went to town on Ennis, creating a suction so tight I had him roaring in pleasure. I reached my hand between my own legs where I was still in the water and found my pussy slick with excitement.

"Fuck, baby, I'm gonna come," Ennis growled. "Take it all, baby, I want you to take all my cum."

I was working myself while sucking him, his dirty words pushing me over the edge. I swallowed all he had for me and trembled through my own orgasm.

Moments later, Stone and Hugh reached down and pulled me out of the pool. Stone led me back to his lounge chair, gesturing toward it with his chin.

"Kneel," he demanded

I wasn't going to argue.

He reached for his blue jeans and retrieved a condom, which he quickly pulled over his erection.

"Spread your legs a little baby," he said, pushing my head down onto the lounge's cushion where my wet hair spread out over it.

His burning gaze ran over my most private parts as I kneeled with my ass high up in the air, followed by his fingers, which gently opened my swollen lips.

"So pink. And so wet," he murmured

"Lookin' good, isn't she?" Hugh growled.

Stone crouched and ran his tongue through my folds, from clit to ass and back. I looked back between my legs, where I watched his enormous cock bounce up and down while he lapped me.

I'd never seen one so huge. Seriously. Like how did he walk around with that thing?

With his face between my legs, he continued to work on my clit while he slipped one, then two fingers inside me. He gently worked them around the inside of my pussy.

Then, he stood, positioning his cock head where his fingers had just been, and entered me just a bit.

But that tiny bit was still huge, and I caught my breath.

"You okay, baby?" he asked, running his hands all over my ass and hips.

I took a deep breath. "More. I want more," I mumbled.

So he pushed further inside me, stretching me to my limits, but so slowly that the initial discomfort passed in seconds.

Fuck, he felt good.

Shaking my ass, I pushed back on him until he was nearly all the way inside me. I bit my lip to keep from crying out, but the second time he drove into me, there was no holding back. I moaned and screamed with the pleasure he was giving me, arching my back to put my ass higher in the air.

God, I loved his cock.

I rocked back and forth as he slammed into me, the lounge chair beneath me tested to its limits. The sun had dried the pool water off me, and I was beginning to sweat. The result was a mixture of my perfume, chlorine, and sex.

With one final push that nearly threw me off the chair, Stone found his own release with a loud growl-groan.

I collapsed on the lounge chair, and Stone joined me, wrapping his arms around me to spoon.

"Holy fuck, that was hot," he said, kissing the back of my neck.

"Jesus. You're not kidding," Ennis said, grabbing a seat on the chair across from us.

"Oh my god, guys. You are so amazing." Once I'd caught my breath, I pushed myself up from the chair and squinted in the sun. "I'm sorry. I'm just completely out of gas."

Stone leaned down and kissed my forehead. "C'mon. I'll take you to bed."

The last thing I remembered was Stone pulling a fluffy comforter over me in his room.

"I'll wake you in an hour for dinner, baby," he said, closing the door behind himself while I fell asleep wearing a smile. There would be time later for worrying about all the crap swirling around Dirty Bandit's life.

And my life, as well.

## 39

HUGH

The moment of truth. We were on our way to meet with the record label. Today was the day they'd tell us what was up.

Could be good news. Could be bad news.

We'd know in a few minutes. In the meantime, it felt like little ants were crawling under my skin, trying to find a way out, and my mouth was so damn dry that no amount of the bottled water I sucked down was touching it. If we got dumped by the label, fine, we'd contract with another. They might not be as prestigious or have as many resources, but who knew, maybe we'd be happier with the change.

On the other hand, the label might have come to

their senses and realized that, even with all our crazy baggage, Dirty Bandit was a fucking music machine that was making their fat-ass execs a shit-ton of money.

Who walks away from a shit-ton of money?

I'm not going to lie. I was edgy as fuck. And I could tell Stone and Ennis were, too. They weren't saying a word, just staring out the limousine windows as we neared downtown LA.

I hadn't been so wound up since the first stadium concert we'd played way back when. The first time you do it, well, it's pretty fucking intense, staring out at literally thousands of people stretching so far into the distance you couldn't even make out their faces. You know how you want good seats at a concert because otherwise you can't see the band? Well, we can't see you, either. And I didn't like that.

When we'd left Ennis's house, I'd grabbed the seat right next to Coral in the car. The other guys could just get over it. I needed her calm confidence, even if she were faking it. I took her hand and held it tight. Bryan, with Pixie in tow, saw and smiled.

I didn't give a shit.

I was hooked. We didn't know yet whether Coral would accept us three guys. It was entirely up to her, and we had no plans to pressure her. But wondering what choice she'd make, and what was up with the record label, was enough to make a grown man want to cry.

*Want* to cry. I didn't *actually* cry.

After an agonizing ride through hellacious LA traffic, we arrived and were ushered into a fancy conference room with floor to ceiling windows offering some of the most expensive views in all of downtown LA. Which I'm sure was paid for to a great extent by the hard work of Dirty Bandit.

A pretty admin came by offering fancy pastries and high-end coffee. She was followed by two men and one woman, all dressed in suits that even my rock 'n roll ass could tell were pretty fucking high end.

Bryan cleared his throat. "Good to see you."

What a set-up. I mean, how is it that we had to answer to a bunch of suits who didn't know a goddamn thing about music except that it could make them money? Who the hell appointed them gatekeepers?

My resentment simmered. These people didn't have a creative bone in their bodies, and their only passion was for making as much money as they possibly could. They produced nothing but their own wealth.

What a boring life that must be. Christ, I could be homeless on the street one day, but I could always play a song on my guitar. Without their bank accounts, these people had nothing and were nothing.

To calm myself, I took a peek at Coral, who sat with a beatific smile, as composed as she'd ever been with her red hair twisted into a knot on top of her head and her pink dress bringing the only color into the room.

I took a deep breath and let my mind wander back to our session by the pool just the day before.

*Focus, asshole.*

The first Suit cleared his throat, signaling that he was about to speak and that he expected everyone's attention.

*Imperious douche.*

He smiled with his overly-whitened teeth. "We wanted to let you know we appreciate the efforts you've been making to be more public-facing. We know it has been a lot of work and hasn't been without its ups and downs"—he paused to look at Stone, and then Ennis—"but we believe you are on the right track. We are interested in continuing our working relationship if we can get these couple issues resolved."

*How kind of them.*

We three guys just sat looking at The Suits. What a contrast we were to them, in our faded concert T-shirts, scruffy blue jeans, and in my case, tattered old flip-flops and a surplus army jacket.

*I wasn't getting dressed up for anyone who thought they could throw us away so easily.*

"Big of you guys," Stone snarled.

Used to his snarky remarks, they just smiled while one of the other Suits leaned onto the table with an elbow. "We have an additional proposition for you," he said, looking directly at Coral.

She sat regally in her chair, ready for anything they

could throw her way. She was not of their world, but she sure knew how to maneuver through it.

Another reason to love her.

Shit. Did I just say *love*?

"What would that be?" she asked sweetly.

The Suit cleared his throat. "This isn't something we'd normally discuss in a group. But since your firm is retained by Dirty Bandit, we need them to be in on the conversation."

What the hell was he getting at?

"We'd like you to come work for the record label. Head up our PR department."

## 40

# HUGH

Coral just looked at him blankly. No reaction whatsoever. But I knew her well enough to know she was about ready to fall off her chair.

"Thank you. That's very flattering—"

The female Suit held up her hand. "Coral, before you say anything, just think about it. I'd be happy to discuss the particulars with you. I think you'll find our compensation package very generous."

I bet. Dicks.

Bryan stood, extending his hand. His earlier forced smile was now long gone. "Thank you, everyone. We need to get to work, so if you'll excuse us, we'll be on our way."

Trying to poach Coral was not making these people any friends.

In the limo on the way home, I turned to Coral. "So. What did you think? You know, of their proposition?"

She looked out the window, shaking her head. "Do they think I want to babysit rock stars all day long? Working with you guys has already taken several years off my life." She dropped her head back and laughed the way I loved.

"Say, Coral, since people are throwing job offers at you, what do you say to coming to work for the band?" Bryan looked around at all of us, and we nodded.

This time, Coral was not as composed. Her eyes widened. "Oh… um… well, that's an interesting offer."

After her non-answer, she sank back in her seat, scrolling through her phone. But I knew the wheels were turning.

When the limo dropped us back at Ennis's house, Bryan headed for his car. "Hey, guys, I gotta take off. Pixie has a playdate. But Coral, think about my offer. I'm sure we can work something out with Randall. We'd love to have you join us."

That's not all we wanted her to join.

Ennis settled into the sofa after opening an expensive bottle of scotch. "Well, that was an interesting meeting."

It might have been early to celebrate, but I felt like we'd walked through the fire. At least the first ring of it.

Coral nodded slowly. "I'd definitely say it was positive. Our work is paying off, but we have more to do. They weren't entirely committed." She sipped her drink. "But I have something else to discuss."

Everyone stopped what they were doing and turned to her. Another situation that could be good news or bad. But really, as long as she was in our lives, we'd be happy. She didn't have to be with us *per se*. Working with us would be enough. If she were happy, we'd be happy.

"I… I've thought over your offer, of you know, being *with* you guys." She looked at each of us, one by one. "It sounds so complicated."

I jumped in. "It doesn't have to be…" Shit. I didn't want to sound desperate.

"Coral, we don't want to pressure you. Our first priority is to make sure you are happy. So, whatever decision you make, we will support," Ennis added.

She got to her feet. "I care about each of you. So much," she said, looking from one of us to the other.

"But I feel compelled to choose *one* of you. Just one. And there's no way I can do that. I want to continue working together. I know we can do great things. But as for being in a relationship… I can't." She looked down at her hands.

"I just can't."

My stomach sank, and the expensive scotch I was sipping was suddenly nauseating. I couldn't look at the other guys, but it was safe to say we all felt like the air had just left the room.

Before I could even think of a way to compose myself and say something, Ennis's doorbell rang several times in a row with an urgency not used by a casual visitor.

"Who's that?" he murmured as he crossed the room to the front door.

"Delivery for you," a perky voice sang. "Sign right here, Sir."

"What the hell is that?" Stone asked, craning his neck to see the large white envelope Ennis returned with.

He studied it for a moment, then passed it to Coral. "It's for you. Maybe something from the office?"

She turned it over, frowning. "Huh. I don't know. There's no return address."

Sighing, she tore into it, pulling out another, smaller envelope. When she'd opened that, she pulled out several photographs. As she shuffled through them, her face turned deadly white and her bottom lip quivered. A small slip of paper fluttered out of the pile and to the floor.

Glancing at it from where she sat, she gasped.

"What is it, sweetie?" I asked, walking over to her.

Holy fuck.

I took the photos from her limp hand. It was clear now why she looked like she might get sick.

I passed them over to the other guys. After rifling

through them, Ennis dropped his head into his hands. Stone jumped to his feet and threw them, scattering them all over the living room.

Which really just made things worse, because we were now looking at a collage of images of all four of us, naked, in and out of the pool, with Coral blowing and fucking us.

Holy fucking shit.

I picked up the piece of paper that had landed on the floor near her foot:


*Hey slut. Looks like you enjoyed being tag teamed by the guys. Maybe you should make sure you're really alone before the next time you act as their cum dumpster.*

## 41

## CORAL

I couldn't breathe.

The room spun around me, and as it did, Hugh's, Ennis's, and Stone's faces morphed into one horrifying deformity of all their features, like some sort of dystopian nightmare.

All I could hear was the blood rushing through my ears, and my stomach was hinting it might reject the couple sips of scotch I'd just consumed.

I somehow got to my feet. I wasn't sure where the guys were, or what they were doing, but I ran out the door to my car and somehow managed to turn the key and drive down the hill. When I reached the bottom, I turned onto Sunset Boulevard and pulled into the first strip mall I saw. I grabbed a parking spot in a far corner and doubled over in my seat, sobbing.

What had I done?

Actually, that was a stupid question. I knew what I'd done. In one passionate, thoughtless moment, I'd ruined my career, the reputation of the agency, and the future of Dirty Bandit.

Worst of all, I'd humiliated myself. Beyond repair.

Why had I fallen prey to my passions, and the guys' flattering attention? Was it vanity, trying to prove to myself—or them—that my awkward, painful years were so far behind me I could take risks and there'd be no penalty to pay?

Or had the guys really grown on me, getting under my skin and into my heart?

It didn't matter. There was no future for us. There never had been.

I took a look at the text messages that had begun to roll in the moment I'd driven away from the house.

*coral, c'mon, let's talk about this*

*you don't have to run off, sweetie*

*where did you go? please, let's talk*

I deleted them as fast as I could, and after twenty more minutes of bawling like a baby, I rummaged through my glove box for some napkins. Wiping the runny mascara off my face, I looked in my rear-view mirror to find I was nothing but a red, swollen, snotty mess.

Deep breath.

I needed to get my shit together and begin damage control. After all, I *was* a PR professional.

Even if I were a huge *slut*.

I sat there in that parking lot, watching people go to and from the bakery, dry cleaner, and mani-pedi salon —people just going about their business, doing their best to get through their errands, and get back to their lives.

My problems weren't any worse than theirs.

So why was I sitting in my car, crying? And feeling sorry for myself?

I knew—we all knew—who was behind the rumors about Stone, the nasty story about Ennis, and now the photos of all of us together.

There was no doubt it had been Carr Evanston.

I'd hoped to sneak into the office unnoticed. I just wasn't in the mood for coworker small talk.

But that was not to be.

"Well, look who it is," Lucy snarled as she stared me down in the hallway. "I was wondering if you were ever coming back to the office, you've been so busy with your *important* client."

I usually tried to think of something nice to say to her snarky, jealousy-fueled, office-bitch remarks, but now they just rubbed me the wrong way. And raised the hairs on the back of my neck.

So I said the nicest thing I could think of. "Lucy, you have lipstick on your teeth."

I brushed past her and headed straight for Randall's office.

"Coral!" he called when he saw me. "How's our resident superstar?"

If he only knew.

"Hey, Randall. Things have been crazy. But I wanted to catch you up."

He smiled, his kind eyes causing a lump in my throat. The last thing in the world I wanted to do was disappoint this man who'd believed in me from the start and given me opportunities I'd never have gotten at another firm.

Of course, I'd worked my ass off for him, and I planned to continue to. Unless he were still planning to bail on Dirty Bandit.

"Remember I told you about that trouble-making journalist, Carr Evanston?" I asked.

He smacked his head like he'd forgotten something. "He's really made some trouble for the band, hasn't he?"

Randall didn't know the half of it.

I nodded, my gaze wandering out the window behind him to the Hollywood Hills, where I'd left the guys so hastily. "Yes he has. And if he continues, we'll have real trouble. The band and I met with the label this morning, and while they were encouraging, they want to see things go more smoothly."

He nodded. "That shouldn't be a problem."

My head snapped in his direction. "What do you mean?"

I didn't know whether to be thrilled or afraid. Randall knew a lot of people. Some on the up-and-up. Others not so much.

"Let's just say, I have a friend who found Evanston. He will be having a... talk with him."

I didn't want to know how Randall had made any of that happen.

But I did want to know if he was satisfied that the rumors about the band members were lies.

"So... are you saying you are no longer considering dumping Dirty Bandit as a client?" I asked.

He frowned at me. "I wouldn't put it that way, Coral. I don't dump clients. But, yes, I am comfortable keeping them on our client roster."

What a relief.

I'd think that meant no more illicit backyard photos, either.

"Um, do you know when your friend will... have the talk with him? Or did he already?"

Randall leaned forward on his desk. "Not sure. Why? Did something else happen?"

God, I wanted to level with Randall. He deserved to know the whole story. But I couldn't let on that I'd been intimate with the guys.

And that I couldn't wait to do it again.

"No, no. Well, it does seem like someone has been, um, snooping around Ennis's house."

He sat back in his chair. "Really? What makes you say that?"

I shrugged, doing my best to keep my cool. "Someone dropped off some photos of the guys... partying in the backyard. They were quite upset."

"No kidding. Well, let me get in touch with my contact and get an update."

"Wonderful, Randall. Thank you. The guys will be thrilled."

As would I.

I stood to head back to my desk, which was by now probably covered in dust—it had been so long since I'd happened by the office.

And as I suspected, my office was a mess. It seems like a universal truth that if you're not on site regularly to defend your territory—in my case, my office—it becomes a dumping ground for all office crap. I sighed as I lifted an old, dead printer off my chair and headed toward the storage closet where it could enjoy its slumber unbothered.

But as I neared the closet, I heard a voice coming from the other side of the door. I was about to knock but stopped when I heard Lucy say my name.

## 42

CORAL

"Coral's in the office right now, and it looks like no one was home this morning. Did you get the new cameras installed? You should have seen the pictures we got yesterday. They were all over each other. She's so busted."

Cameras? What cameras?

"Okay, great. I'll have cash for you tonight. The great thing is, Carr, they're going to go crazy trying to figure out who did it, since you supposedly have called it quits."

Holy shit.

Lucy was behind the photos taken of me with the guys? And she was working with Carr?

No fucking way. Was she crazy? Was he?

Actually, I was pretty sure they both were.

I hustled back to my office, where I dumped the printer in the corner and quickly texted the guys.

*there are cameras planted in ennis's backyard. be careful*

I sat at my desk, trying to think of next steps, and ran back to the closet.

She was still in there.

I hit *record* on my phone and held it to the door, fingers crossed that Randall wouldn't happen by and start asking questions.

"Oh yeah, they got copies of yesterday's photos today. What? No, I'm not going to the press with them unless they won't pay. Seriously, Carr, as soon as we get our cash, we're fucking out of here. I hate this firm, my asshole boss, and his pet, Coral. Although, once they pay us, we could still publish the shit we gather. Just to fuck with them."

She let out a long cackle and said goodbye.

I turned and made like I was just walking down the hall.

"Hey, Lucy. How are the shoe clients?" I asked pleasantly, although I was fantasizing about tearing her eyes out.

What a fucking loon. A fury rose in me that not only was she trying to fuck me over, but also that she was so willing to hurt others with her crazy mission.

She wasn't going to get away with it. She'd hurt the guys over my dead body.

"Oh, hey, Coral," she said, looking startled.

Yeah, she was wondering if I'd heard her. And I'd let her continue to wonder. For a while, at least.

"I was thinking. Would you like to meet the guys of Dirty Bandit some time? They're super hot and lots of fun."

Tormenting her was going to be one of my greatest pleasures.

She stopped short, her eyes lighting up. "Really? Do you think I could?"

Wow. After throwing those guys under the bus, she could really go hang out with them and pretend to be friends?

She was more of a bitch than I thought.

I smiled sweetly. "Of course. I'm sure they'll like you. Let me call them real quick, and I'll get back to you."

She held her head up smugly, certain she was the one coming out ahead.

She had no freaking idea.

I accompanied Lucy to her office and glanced at my phone. "Oh crap, I'm late for a meeting with Randall. But I'll call the guys right after and we'll go up to the Hills, okay? Don't go home without me!"

I had to keep her in the office.

She looked like a kid in a candy store. "Okay. And Coral—thank you."

Yeah, she'd really be thanking me soon.

"Oh, hi, Coral. You're back. What's up?" Randall asked.

I took a deep breath. "I have some very important things to share with you, Randall."

So I started at the beginning and played the recorded conversation I'd captured. To say Randall was blown away was an understatement.

"Well, fuck me," he said, looking around his office in shock. "This is horrible on so many levels. I always wondered what was so strange about Lucy, but to think she'd hurt so many people just because she was a jealous nut bag. Christ, I never saw it coming."

I had to keep Randall on track. Time was of the essence, and I didn't want Lucy wondering why I was taking so long with him.

He put his head in his hands.

"Randall," I said to grab his attention, "you need to act like nothing is up. I'll go get her right now. You keep her occupied for a few minutes."

He nodded. "I got it. Let's go."

I ran back to Lucy's office, where I found her scrolling through her phone with her usual bitch smile.

"Lucy!" I said urgently. "Randall needs you right now. Some sort of emergency."

Her eyes bugged. "Oh my god. I wonder what's up?"

She dropped her phone on her desk and ran out her office door.

Bingo.

I grabbed her phone before it locked and while walking back to my office, scrolled to see if she had an app for her spy cameras.

She did.

God, I wanted to kill her.

Next, I looked in her photo library, where she stored the videos of the guys and me. I forwarded them all to myself and dropped her phone into my purse. Let her search high and low for the damn thing.

Then I grabbed my bag and headed out.

But before I did, I ran into Lucy returning to her desk. I walked alongside her until we reached her office.

"What did Randall need?" I asked innocently.

She shrugged. "Nothing really. Hey, are we heading up to see the band right now?" she asked, turning off her computer and grabbing her purse.

She looked around her desk like something was missing.

Yeah, bitch, something sure was missing from your desk.

"I am. Randall's coming up in a few. Catch a ride with him?"

She nodded and continued to push things around on her desk as I headed to the parking garage.

"Hey, Coral," she called after me, "have you seen my phone?"

I turned to face her, walking backwards. "I think you had it when you went into Randall's office. Gotta run!"

I got in my car and headed into the Hills. I had a few things to share with the guys and this time it was all good news.

## 43

## STONE

I'd never seen a prettier sight.

Coral came blasting into the house with about the biggest goddamn smile I'd ever seen her wearing.

Which was funny because Hugh, Ennis, and I were sulking in the living room wondering what the hell was up with her, especially after we'd gotten her text that there were spy cameras in Ennis's backyard.

Fucking people. They'll stop at nothing to ruin your life.

"Guys," she blurted out, jumping up and down like a little kid, "you won't freaking believe what's going on. Get ready, because the next hour or two of our lives are going to be a wild ride."

Hugh looked hopeful, Ennis was skeptical, and I was just having a great fucking time.

Bring it on, baby.

Coral called one of those security technicians who could locate hidden cameras, and he was on his way up to the house. Her boss would follow later with someone named Lucy, who apparently was going to be in for some big surprises.

It'd be a regular party.

Coral gathered up the photos that had sent her reeling just a few hours before and stuffed them back in their envelope. She set the IT technician to work in the yard as soon as he arrived, and sat down with us while we waited for our plan to fall into place.

The guys and I were upset about the photos of course, but even more upset for Coral's sake. An invasion of privacy like that would be hard on her, and we felt terrible.

We also felt like shit that a relationship with her was not in the cards. But at least she'd still be around to work with us.

And I planned to continue to admire her curvy ass and bouncy little tits. No harm in that, right?

She sat on the edge of the sofa and waved her hands around. "So, I have more news for you guys—"

"Oh, hey, all done," the IT guy said, coming in from the backyard and setting some very small electronics on the coffee table in front of us.

Those little pieces of shit were responsible for so many of our problems?

He hitched his pants and pushed his glasses up on his nose. "Amateurs."

"What?" Hugh asked. "Can you elaborate?"

He picked up one of the devices and turned it over with his fingers.

"Damn things. Such wonders of technology, capable of so much destruction."

He could say that again.

"Whoever installed them wasn't too smart. I found them in seconds. I got 'em all, though. You're safe now. But you might want to get some security for the house. Here's my card," he said with a smile.

Coral showed him to the door, paid him, and he left.

"Wow. Look at these little things," Ennis said, pushing them around the table. "Anyway, Coral, you were saying you had something else to discuss?"

She took a seat and slapped her palms on her thighs. "Yes. I do. I've been thinking—"

Just then, the doorbell rang.

"Oh gosh," she said, grabbing the cameras and sweeping them into the vase on the table. "That would be Randall and Lucy. Don't let on anything."

She sprinted to the door and opened it with an expansive *hello*.

"Hey, guys," Randall said, extending his hand. "It's been a while, hasn't it?"

We all stood and greeted Randall as cordially as possible. After all, it was he who'd introduced Coral to our lives.

"Guys, this is my coworker, Lucy. She's a big fan," Coral said gleefully.

Guess she was about to find out what sort of fan Coral was of *hers*.

Lucy looked like she would blow away in a stiff wind, she was so skinny. She clapped her hands together and beamed. "Oh my god. I'm so excited. I can't believe I'm meeting you guys right here at one of your homes."

She shook all our hands and paused when she got to me, taking one of mine in both of hers.

Shit. She was one of *those*.

Back in the day, I'd have fucked a girl like her. It was easy to see she'd be a pain in the ass for anything more than a one-nighter. She'd probably expect to hear from me after she'd given me her phone number, and she'd watch her text messages for a couple weeks. Then she'd realize that she'd never see my ass again—at least not in person.

Yeah, I knew her type.

But that shit was behind me, and now that I was seeing the world a little differently, I realized what a dick I'd been to all the Corals of the world.

And there were a shit-ton of them out there.

Never too late to turn over a new leaf though, right?

Ennis sidled up to Lucy, tearing her attention away

from me. It was all I could do not to chuckle out loud. "Lucy, can I show you around? We have a gorgeous yard with a pool. In fact, maybe you'd like to come by sometime for a swim?"

Her smile faded, replaced by nervousness. "Oh, that would be nice. But I don't really swim."

Ennis ushered her outside like the perfect host.

"So were the cameras found?" Randall asked quietly.

"Yeah. They're in there," Coral said, pointing toward the vase.

He peeked inside. "Damn. There's nothing to them."

Then, he looked at us guys. "I'm so sorry this was someone from our team. I don't know how I'll make it up to you."

Shit, I could think of one big way he could make it up to us.

"Well, there's one idea, Randall," Coral said. "They'd like to hire me directly."

She put her hand on his arm as if to comfort him. But it wasn't necessary.

He thought for a moment. "Wow. That could be an incredible opportunity for you, Coral," he said.

Surprise washed over her face. "Really? You're not mad? Are you sure?"

He put his hands up. "Look, I would be very, very sad to lose you. But I know we'll continue to work together, and besides, think of all the celebrity clients you can throw my way."

She burst out laughing. "My god, Randall. Do you ever stop thinking about business?"

She had his number, and it was clear that was one of the things he adored about her.

"No, I don't suppose I do," he said.

"Well, that's why you're so successful," she said, playfully slapping his arm.

Hugh craned his neck to see the backyard. "Christ, Ennis is really laying it on."

We all looked in his direction. He had an arm around Lucy's shoulder and was pointing out the various LA neighborhoods in the distance.

Coral popped out of her seat. "I think I hear the cops," she said.

Cops? What the hell?

Hugh and I looked at each other, then at Randall and Coral.

"Just watch this, guys," she said.

She pulled the door open and a man and woman from LAPD entered. "Thank you for coming," she said graciously.

I wasn't a big fan of cops, but it was nice to have them on my side for a change.

It seemed they'd already been briefed about what was going on. How Coral pulled that off was beyond me.

Randall leaned out the patio doors. "Lucy, there's someone here to see you."

She turned around with wide eyes, clearly counting

on meeting some other celebrity. Pushing Ennis's arm off her shoulders, she came skipping back to the house.

But she stopped short when she saw the police.

"Um. Who did you want me to meet?" she asked with an uneasy smile, looking around the room.

Coral dumped the cameras out of the vase, pulled a cell phone from her purse, grabbed the envelope of photos, and laid it all on the coffee table.

Lucy turned dead white. "Oh guys, I've got to get back to the office. It was great meeting you all," she said, heading toward the door.

But the female cop stepped right in front of her. "Ma'am, not so fast."

Anger splashed across her face. "What? No way," she said, charging for the door.

But the cops caught her by the arms and began reading her rights.

When they were done, Coral approached her. "Lucy, we know you made illegal videos of Ennis's backyard and sent these printed photos to shake us down. I found the images on your phone. I also recorded you speaking with Carr Evanston. You both will have to answer for this."

Lucy screwed her face up while the cops escorted her out. "Fuck you, Coral. Fuck you, too, Randall. You guys never gave me a chance."

Damn.

On the way out, I patted Lucy on the back. "Keep your chin up, honey. Jail food ain't too bad."

"Shut up!" she screamed.

The cops shook their heads and ushered her out.

I turned back to the group, and Coral and Randall were shaking with laughter. Finally, they couldn't keep it quiet any longer and howled until they couldn't breathe.

44

**STONE**

"Okay, everybody. I've started this conversation multiple times and we keep getting interrupted," Coral said after her boss left.

"Crazy day, huh, sweetie?" I said.

Christ, was I glad all the bullshit about Ennis and me had been put to bed. Imagine. Lucy in cahoots with that creep Carr Evanston.

And now they were both going to jail.

Fools.

All because Carr was bent out of shape that I'd punched his lights out a long time ago, and Lucy was jealous of Coral and her success.

What a couple of losers.

Coral kicked off her shoes.

She sure was making herself comfortable for someone who wasn't sticking around.

Or was that what she had to talk to us about?

"What's on your mind, gorgeous?" Hugh said, just drinking all of her in.

I had a feeling there'd be a lot of that, since we weren't going to really *be with* her any longer.

She took a deep breath. "Well, guys, I thought really hard about some things today—undoubtedly one of the craziest days of my life."

We waited.

"I'd like you to know that… I want to stay," she blurted out.

"Great," Hugh said, clapping his hands together. "We're thrilled you're going to work for the band. Bryan will be psyched."

Her eyes widened. "Oh, well, yes. There's that."

"Yeah, Bryan will be very happy," I added.

"Have you told him yet?" Ennis asked.

She nodded, then shook her head. "Yeah. I mean no. No, I haven't talked to Bryan yet. But I *am* on board to work for Dirty Bandit. I'm also on board for something else."

We guys looked at each other like the confused dumbasses we were.

"Guys," she said pointedly, "I want to be with you. All of you. I think we can make it work."

We looked at each other in disbelief.

"Did you guys just hear what I did?" I said.

Hugh jumped to his feet and grabbed Coral, swinging her in a circle.

She squealed with delight, and turned to Ennis to plant a big one on his lips.

When they lingered for a moment too long, I tapped my friend and bandmate on the shoulder. "Dude. Step aside," I said, and he did.

I wove my fingers deep into Coral's hair, pulling her to my mouth, and kissing her so hard I knew her lips would be sore the next day—I couldn't help it, I just needed to mark her in some primitive way.

"Oh my god!" she said when I finally released her. "What shall we do to celebrate?"

We looked at each other and laughed, dropping our clothes to the floor and running for the pool.

None of us knew what the future held—successful albums and sold-out concerts, or not—but we'd keep making good music one way or the other, thanks to the love of our amazing Coral.

Did you like *Her Dirty Rockers*? Check out the next
book in the Men at Work series,
*Her Dirty Teachers*

I hope you loved reading this book as much as I loved writing it.
Please visit my store to learn more about my books, and to buy directly from me!
https://mikalaneshop.com/

SHOP
Mika
Lane

Dear Reader:

I'm USA TODAY bestselling romance author Mika Lane, and am OBSESSED with bringing you sassy, steamy stories with imperfect heroines and the bad-a*s dudes they bring to their knees. I'll always bring you my signature humor and heat, topped off with a modern-day happily ever after.

My first book ever was *The Day I Ate the Milkyway*, a true fourth-grade masterpiece illustrated with crayons and bound with construction paper and glue. Nowadays, steamy romance gives purpose to my days and nights as I create worlds and characters that tickle the imagination. I live in magical Northern California with my own handsome alpha dude, sometimes known as Mr. Mika Lane, and two devilish cats named Chuck and Murray.

A dual citizen of the United States and Ireland, I have on more than one occasion spent my last dollar on a plane ticket somewhere, and am always planning my next escape. I often try new recipes on unsuspecting friends, search out hiding places to read undisturbed, and sadly kill every houseplant I bring home.

I LOVE to hear from readers when I'm not dreaming up naughty tales to share. Visit my online shop https://mikalaneshop.com/ and say hello https://mikalaneshop.com/pages/meet-mika.

xoxo, Mika